The Rest Is Slander

SEAGULL
BOOKS
•
CELEBRATING
40 YEARS

THE GERMAN LIST

THOMAS BERNHARD

The Rest Is Slander

Five Stories

Translated by Douglas Robertson

LONDON NEW YORK CALCUTTA

GOETHE INSTITUT

This publication has been supported by a grant from
the Goethe-Institut India

Seagull Books, 2024

The following stories were originally published
in German by Suhrkamp Verlag, Frankfurt am Main:

'On the Ortler: A Message from Gomagoi', published as 'Am Ortler'.
© Suhrkamp Verlag, Frankfurt am Main, 1971.

'Midland at Stilfs', published as 'Midland in Stilfs'.
© Suhrkamp Verlag, Frankfurt am Main, 1971.

'The Weatherproof Cape', published as 'Der Wetterfleck'.
© Suhrkamp Verlag, Frankfurt am Main, 1971.

'Ungenach', published as 'Ungenach'.
© Suhrkamp Verlag, Frankfurt am Main, 1968.

All rights reserved by and controlled through Suhrkamp Verlag Berlin.

'At the Timberline' was originally published as 'An der Baumgrenze',
© Residenz Verlag, Salzburg, 1969.

English translation © Douglas Robertson, 2022
First published in English by Segaull Books, 2022

ISBN 978 1 8030 9 449 6

British Library Cataloguing-in-Publication Data
A catalogue record for this book is available from the British Library

Typeset by Seagull Books, Calcutta, India
Printed and bound by WordsWorth India, New Delhi, India

CONTENTS

TRANSLATOR'S ACKNOWLEDGEMENTS

The translator wishes to extend his sincerest thanks to flowerville for her invaluable insight and assistance in reviewing the complete preliminary draft of the translation.

ON THE ORTLER

A Message from Gomagoi

In the middle of October we set out on the path leading from Gomagoi to a chalet that had been left to us by our parents thirty-five years earlier, to a small pasture-framed stonework farmhouse on the Scheibenboden beneath the Ortler massif; our intention had been to spend two, three years together up on the Scheibenboden, undisturbed and entirely alone, preoccupied with our experiences and ideas and with thoughts about a world that as far as I, now in my forty-eighth year, was concerned, and my brother, now in his fifty-first year, was concerned, no longer had anything to do with us. The farmhouse, situated eighteen hundred metres above sea level, seemed, as far as we had learnt or still remembered, to be superlatively well suited to our purposes, about which we had uttered nothing to a single human being, because we wished to keep our project absolutely secret and not to imperil it by divulging as much as a single one of its particulars or engaging in any impertinent and ill-considered chit-chat and because we did not wish to be taken for fools. One reason, not the ultimate one, my dear sir, for our reactivating the farmhouse on the Scheibenboden had been the idea of the extraordinary cheapness of an existence in the mountains, an existence devoid of human beings and therefore devoid of distractions. Well-equipped and with at least eight or ten days' provisions in our rucksacks (in the light of our plan, our intention vis-à-vis our property on the Scheibenboden had first and foremost been to move into the chalet at the beginning of November, to begin a rational inspection of it, to take a good, close look at it with a view to its inhabitability), we put Gomagoi behind us at four in the morning; the night was clear; we had no need of our English lamps, and thanks to our taciturnity and immersed as we were in our single incessant and fascinating and absolutely fettering idea—no commitments, no scientific expertise, on the one hand, and our fantastic undertaking on the other—we made very speedy progress. But soon, my dear sir, thanks to a sudden handful of remarks on an entirely different topic, it became evident that although we were exclusively preoccupied with our enterprise, with the chalet on the Scheibenboden as a goal, we were nevertheless unfit for bipartite taciturnity, that we would be obliged to suspend our taciturnity with several remarks regarding something entirely different, and all of a sudden we were engaged in a remarkable conversation, a conversation that we initially found irritating but soon acclimatized ourselves to completely and that not least caused us to feel a kind of abhorrent delight, a conversation about the object of our life, or, rather, the object of our existence, my dear sir, a conversation which on account of its fragmentary character and quite close topical connection with my brother's palpably degenerative illness and with the changes in my own person induced by the degenerativeness of my brother's illness, a conversation that probably requires analysis by an entirely different person than myself, a conversation that will also be of engrossing interest to you, as of course throughout his life, and not only in your capacity as his agent, you were in contact with my brother as no other human being was. We, who were already quite some distance from Gomagoi, were suddenly conversing with each other in the following manner: whenever you have been rehearsing one of your feats of acrobatic artistry, I said to my brother, who, as you know, did nothing but rehearse feats of acrobatic artistry throughout his life, I have always been obliged to think of your feat of acrobatic artistry as a life-imperilling feat of acrobatic artistry; complementarily, you, whenever I have been preparing my scholarly work (on atmospheric strata), have been obliged to think of my scholarly work as life-imperilling. And so all our lives, while you have been rehearsing your feats of acrobatic artistry and I have been preparing my scholarly work (on atmospheric strata), our lives have constantly been imperilled, I said. And yet we don't ask ourselves, he said, how we ever came by our feats of acrobatic artistry, how we ever came by our scholarly work (on atmospheric strata), and how I came by my feats of acrobatic artistry (both on the ground and on the tightrope) and how you came by your scholarly work (on atmospheric strata), etc. And how we perfected our feats of acrobatic artistry and how we perfected our scholarly work, etc., he said. At first, he said, he had believed he would never succeed at performing his feat of acrobatic artistry, any feat of acrobatic artistry whatsoever, but then he did succeed at performing it; just as I had believed that I would never successfully produce my scholarly work (on atmospheric strata) and yet I did subsequently succeed in producing it. He must, he said, have always been thinking: *a different, more complicated feat of acrobatic artistry!* and he also always succeeded at performing a different, more complicated feat of acrobatic artistry, just as I invariably succeeded at producing a different (and yet the same) and invariably more complicated and invariably much more complicated scholarly work (and yet always the same scholarly work on atmospheric strata). To begin with, the first feat of acrobatic artistry; then the second feat of acrobatic artistry, then the third, the fourth, the fifth, etc. A redoubling of the exertion applied to the feat of acrobatic artistry, I invariably kept thinking, he said; a redoubling of the exertion applied to the study (of atmospheric strata), I invariably kept saying to myself, I thought. We were now crossing the Trafoier Bach. I quite simply redoubled the exertion and succeeded at performing the feats of acrobatic artistry, he said. Eventually the most complicated feats of acrobatic artistry. You saw that my feats of acrobatic artistry were getting more and more complicated, but you never told me so; I mustn't let him notice it, you were always thinking, I must withhold all that I have been observing, I must betray nothing to him; just as I never told you that I was observing how your scholarly work on atmospheric strata was getting more complicated, and always with ever-increasing interest, with the greatest imaginable degree of attentiveness, the greatest anxiety, etc., he said. At first I thought to myself: *a feat of acrobatic artistry!* and then: *a more complicated feat of acrobatic artistry!* and then: *now the most complicated feat of acrobatic artistry!* Of my head, he said. Your scholarly work, he said, was getting more and more complicated; all those thousands, those hundreds of thousands of sums and figures, he said; thanks to them I was rehearsing ever-more complicated feats of acrobatic artistry. The interdependency of my scholarly work (on atmospheric strata) and his feats of acrobatic artistry was, he said, enormously great. It would someday be necessary to analyse this interdependency, he said and added that our period of residence in the chalet was going to be especially beneficial to such an analysis. Because after all in the chalet we would be unable to be absorbed exclusively in meditation and only ever in nothing but meditation, he said and added that he very strongly wished for us to concretize on paper various points of our body of thought that seemed important to us. Even though we have resolved not to abuse the chalet on the Scheibenboden by engaging in written study there, he said, I have brought along some writing paper, obviously, he said. By dint of study, by dint of uninterrupted observation of your scholarly work on atmospheric strata, he said, little by little, and above all during my period of residence in Zurich, he said, at the same time and in the same proportion as you were perfecting yourself in your study of atmospheric strata, I attained perfection in my feats of acrobatic artistry. A *certain* perfection, he said and immediately added: faster, let us walk faster, the path to the chalet is extremely long, the ascent to the Scheibenboden is extremely long, extremely onerous, as I recall. By dint of specific arm movements as well as leg movements as well as head movements and the regulation thereof, by dint of this specific, forward-racing bodily rhythm, he said, it is possible to walk even faster, to progress even faster; we shall come to progress even faster. He had said this sentence in the exact same tone of voice as that of our father, who at every instant of our earlier ascents of the Ortler had always said the sentence to us, who detested those ascents of the Ortler, in order to keep us moving forward. When you were observing me penetratingly, unrelentingly and penetratingly, said my brother, I was always thinking and when

7

I was always observing you just as penetratingly and unrelentingly, when we were observing each other always unrelentingly and penetratingly with regard to my feats of acrobatic artistry and your scholarly work, each of us was unrelentingly and with an ever-increasing, ever-more ruthless penetrativeness observing *what* the other was doing and *how* he was doing it, constantly observing *what* and *how*, to the very verge of madness, he said, and in so doing we schooled each other throughout our lives. It was all, he said, a question of the art of observation and in the art of observation a question of the ruthlessness of the art of observation and in the ruthlessness of the art of observation a question of the absolute constitution of the intellect. Because we were eventually interested in nothing apart from our feats of acrobatic artistry and our scholarly work, he said, it became impossible in a horrible fashion for us to get along with the people around us, who accordingly punished us with their total lack of interest. The people around us began ignoring us at the precise moment when we ceased to take the slightest interest in them, he said, obviously. To be sure, he asserted, putting up with this state of affairs verged on absolute insufferableness, an ongoing attempt at or ongoing temptation by or ongoing desire for death that we were more intimately familiar with than with anything else. How evenly you always breathed *before* and *after* your feat of acrobatic artistry, I said. Breathing is the most important thing, he said. When one has mastered one's breathing, one has mastered everything. He did not regret having enrolled in this school, this school accredited by nobody besides himself, the school of breathing. One must master one's head, one's thoughts, one's body through breathing, he said, and by mastering breathing alone develop a mastery of the finest of all arts. Initially you believed, I said, that you were not going to be able to master your feat of acrobatic artistry, because you were unable to master breathing, because you couldn't breathe in the fashion appropriate to the feat of acrobatic artistry, because of course one must always be able to breathe in the fashion appropriate to the feat of acrobatic artistry one is hoping to master, that one is rehearsing; one must be able to breathe in a fashion appropriate to the scholarly work, the intellectual work, that one is hoping to master, that one is preparing, he said; breathing is everything, nothing is as important as breathing; the body, and brain can come into their own only through breathing, he said; initially, you cannot master your feat of acrobatic artistry, because you cannot breathe in the manner appropriate to the feat of acrobatic artistry, I said; then you can breathe in the appropriate manner, he said, but you cannot master your feat of acrobatic artistry, this is all a process lasting years, lasting decades, he said, and then you do master your feat of acrobatic artistry, because you have mastered breathing in the manner appropriate to that feat of acrobatic artistry, and you cannot *perform* it! For in every art of everything the art of performance is the most difficult of all arts. You have mastered your feat of acrobatic artistry, but you cannot perform it; there is nothing more depressing, no form of depression that is worse, no state of affairs that is more horrendous, he said. This accounts for the title of my little essay *Acrobatic Artistry and the Art of Performance*, a topic that has preoccupied me all my life, as you know, and a topic that has never ceased to preoccupy me and a topic that always will preoccupy me. All told the very most delicate of all topics, he said, whose power to inspire dread is by no means confined to the so-called artistic world. And what topic should one set about tackling, he said, if not a topic that inspires dread in the entire world. He said he would be so bold as to maintain that the topic of the art of performance in all its modifications was the most important of all topics. For what would, for example, my feats of acrobatic artistry in general amount to without my art of performance and what would, for example, all of philosophy and all of natural science and all of science in general, and all of humanity and all of humankind in general, amount to without the art of performance? he said. I was always setting to work on this essay; at a specific point, a point that fettered me to it, he said, I would set to work on it and develop it and develop it all the way to the stage of its perfection, which at the same time was the stage of its dissolution, of its disaggregation, he said. In this fashion there came into being roughly a hundred essays on this topic, the most astonishing, the most remarkable, the most outrageous conclusions. Granted, a few notes still exist, a few notes, a few topical particles. Essays, he said, basically exist only for the purpose of being annihilated, even an essay on the art of performance, he said. The raison d'être of all essays is doubt about their topic, you understand, is doubting everything, investigatively extracting everything from the darkness and doubting it and annihilating it. Everything. Without exception. Essays are essays that are meant to be annihilated. The difficult thing, he said, is always extracting everything *from the same head*, everything contained in an idea *from a single head, from a single head, from a single brain*, then he added: *using a unique, always the same unique body*. This is the difficulty of displaying or making public the product of the mind or the product of the body, in other words, my feats of acrobatic artistry or your scholarly work, my corporeal art or your intellectual art (mine being on the ground and on the tightrope) and yours on atmospheric strata, without being obliged immediately to commit suicide, the difficulty of undergoing this horrible process of humiliation without killing oneself, of displaying what one is, of making public what one is, he said, of going through the hell of performance and the hell of making something public, of managing to go through this hell, of being obliged to go through this hell, through this hell of performance and through this hell of making something public, of ruthlessly going through this most horrible of all hells. We caught sight of the Payerhütte and my brother said, even though by he was now totally exhausted, *don't slow down, don't, because we are moving uphill, slow down.* He always mimicked Father's utterance of this sentence peerlessly well. *Don't slow down, because we are moving upwards; don't slow down, because we are ascending.* And he added: *keen air! keen air!* like my father. You were always anxious when standing before your feat of acrobatic artistry, I said. Anxious *before* the feat, anxious *after* the feat. Never anxious *during* the feat. Your acrobatic artistry-inspired anxiety, I said. And you were always anxious when standing before your scholarly work, before the results of your researches. Never-ending anxiety, he said. Your scientific anxiety and my acrobatic-artistic anxiety, he said. He relished this expression and he repeated it two, three times, as we began breathing more easily and thereby actually managed to make speedier progress, progress along a path that had been an uphill one for some time. Not *in the middle of* the feat, he said, not *in the middle of* the feat, never anxious *in the middle of* the feat. But your anxiety was perpetual, your anxiety was an unremitting anxiety, he said. And I: and I was always anxious on your behalf as well. During your feats, I said. During my rehearsal of a feat, he said, I was not anxious about suddenly failing to master it, because I was not thinking about that, because I could not think about that; I was rehearsing my feat; during the feat, I was never anxious, but *you* were always anxious when I was rehearsing a feat. In the forest he spoke about how it had all of a sudden ceased to be possible for him to do anything but rehearse his feats of acrobatic artistry, while I spoke about how in the blink of an eye I had ceased to find it possible to do anything but be completely alone with my scholarly work, with atmospheric strata, I said, to have anything to do with anything else. And what was the upshot of that, of what use was it to have the rudiments of a fairly lengthy study in my head, given that I did not have it in my head in *just* the right way I would have needed in order to perform the work of carrying it out, and for this reason it all seemed to boil down to the question: and what is the upshot of this? In an instant I had once again become conscious of the fact that one must not merely be constantly practising, having thoughts and quite simply practising with those thoughts, that one must also be constantly practising being able to express those thoughts at any time, for unexpressed thoughts are nothing. Articulating what he doubtless regarded as a non sequitur, I suddenly said: unexpressed thoughts are nothing. Whereupon he said that it was precisely unexpressed thoughts that were the most important ones, as history had proved. For in every case expressed thoughts were diluted thoughts, and unexpressed thoughts the most efficacious ones. Admittedly also the most devastating ones, he said but added that he would not dwell on this, that such a topic was off-limits to him. From here onwards he only gave an answer that was no answer: the Königsspitze is seen whenever it is seen, but today the Königsspitze isn't seen. Such a reaction and such a sentence coming from him characterized him better than anything else. Because all of a sudden everything in me became concentrated on my feats of acrobatic artistry, I was for the majority of my life the most despair-ridden of human beings, he said. You exist only for your feats of acrobatic artistry and are, in a very strict sense, your feats of acrobatic artistry, I kept repeating to myself. Everything is a feat of acrobatic artistry. Everything is a feat of acrobatic artistry. The entire world is a feat of acrobatic artistry. I said: I have always thought, if only he doesn't fall, if only he doesn't fall to the ground and have a fatal accident and how many years have I been obliged to keep thinking this, I said and you have not fallen to the ground, you have not had a fatal accident. Now we are going to the Scheibenboden, I said, and going up to the chalet. The terminus, the moment is always extremely ridiculous, he said. To think that that we have resolved to go to the Scheibenboden, that we have resolved to visit the chalet, that we ever went back to Gomagoi at all! he said. We sent telegrams, we met up in Gomagoi, we resolved to effect a hiatus in my acrobatic artistry, a hiatus in your scholarly work (on atmospheric strata), all of a sudden we had a crazy plan and we set about realizing this crazy plan and we are now setting about realizing our plan; we are climbing higher and higher, to the Scheibenboden, up to the chalet, he said. A sudden transformation of the state of affairs, he said. The need, as if all the answers were to be found therein, to be all of sudden together again in seclusion and sequestration, because for several decades our time together had been thwarted by disturbances; the will to complete freedom from disturbances, and in fresh air to boot, I said, at the highest of heights. Forsaken abodes, forsaken people, forsaken cities, forsaken projects, every-thing was forsaken. Only once your feat was over and done with did I breathe easily again, I said. And he: Not being anxious at all was what I was afraid of. When you were working on your atmospheric strata and I was thinking, he is working on his atmospheric strata and when I was rehearsing and trying out my feats of acrobatic artistry and you were thinking, he is rehearsing, he is trying out his feat of acrobatic artistry, we were calm. And when we would go into an inn, like Pinggera's, he said, but now we are not going to stop by Pinggera's inn, we shan't stop at Pinggera's inn no matter what and we passed by Pinggera's inn; on the one hand I would have quite liked to stop at Pinggera's inn, on the other hand a visit to an inn at such an early hour of the day would have had a devastating effect on me and on us both; a couple of glasses of schnapps would have had a devas-tating effect in the morning; and when we would go into an inn, like Pinggera's for example, said my brother as we passed by Pinggera's inn, and we were gradually warming up, you would say, *head straight for the corner*, right away: *head straight for the corner*, your habitual utterance, he said, *we can't have our backs to anybody*, your wish. Do you remember? he said and Pinggera's inn was already behind us, into the forest, he said, into the dark-ness, upward, upward, higher, higher. At one point, having briefly drawn to a halt, he said: your experiment with the uni-versity! And I: your experiment with the academy! Then farther, even more rapidly farther; at first they had encumbered us, now our rucksacks no longer encumbered us. And when you were buying shoes, he said, you would ask me whether you should buy the shoes. Are these the appropriate shoes? you would ask.

When you were buying a coat, is this the appropriate coat? What insanity it was, he said, to go to the university, he said and I said: What inanity, what a huge waste of time, the academy. Amid the illnesses, the most dangerous, prolonged illnesses. Unremitting infections, he said. Unremitting corporeal frailty, he said. On the one hand the illnesses of our mother, on the other hand the illnesses of our father. And then illnesses that are illnesses of our mother *and* our father. Entirely new, unresearched illnesses. Always of the greatest interest to all doctors. Monotony. Antipathy. Left on our own very early on, we went to rack and ruin, I said. No protest. And then the feats of acrobatic artistry and then your science and alternately more interest in feats of acrobatic artistry and more interest in science, but always a more intensive interest. Peerlessness. Out of being left on our own and out of our anxiety we fashioned our feats of acrobatic artistry and our science. No assistance. No encouragement. No fortuitous ovations, he said. Our frugality, which came to our assistance. Otherwise nothing, he said. And the art of not thinking about it. Your words, he said: precision, more and more precision, incorruptibility, mental acuity. My words: effects, possibilities of refinement, ostentation. Our joint unremitting contempt for the people around us. Fend them off, turn them away, sever all ties with them, he said. Time and again: in all circumstances, in any weather, in all circumstances. Do you remember? In Basel I was anxious because I thought it might not succeed, in Vienna I was anxious, in Zurich, in St Valentin. Anxious because I thought it might not succeed. Too many people at one time, then too few people at another. Too much attention at one time, then at another: too little attention. Too

much ado, too little ado, too much impatience, too much experience. *Faster, children,* he said, *over the Suldenbach, faster, children,
across the Suldenbach.* I still hear our father. If we say what we
are thinking, he was extremely ruthless; it was something else.
Why did he always box your ears specifically at Pinggera's tavern? I said. *Faster, children, across the Suldenbach, faster, children,
across the Suldenbach.* I still hear my father. The privilege of being
boxed on the ears by our mother instead of by him. My brother
said: only once the two of them were dead did we develop
according to our abilities and according to our needs. After their
death, by an exertion of our own strength of will we dared to
exist our own existence; without parents we were free. No forbearance, he said, no forbearance. No untruth. As I was ailing
and as there was gradually nothing in me but a decline in my
strength. Under the influence of our parents, he said. Can you
still hear, he said, him saying: *faster, children, across the
Suldenbach, faster, children, across the Suldenbach?* No untruth.
No absolution. Their shared ruthlessness and our shared vulner-
ability, he said. No absolution. Their shared despicableness, he
said. *Faster, children, across the Suldenbach.* No forbearance.
Being on the Scheibenboden as a punishment, said my brother
now, going up to the Scheibenboden as a punishment and coming
down from the Scheibenboden as a punishment and walking
through the Suldental as a punishment and walking to Gomagoi
as a punishment, and coming home as a punishment, everything
as a punishment. Our life as a punishment. Our childhood as a
punishment. Everything as a punishment. Suddenly the
Tabaretta Ridge . And then farther through the forest. Do you
remember? Books. Essays—written compositions, *decomposi-
tions.* Parents. Childhood and everything after it. The process of

isolation. Fragments of despair. That time we showed up in Berlin in Hubertus coats. Do you remember? Twenty years with a shoe size that was too small and a head that was too big. The problem has always been an insoluble problem. But farther, onward. Always given the cold shoulder when we got there. I ask, nobody answers. Learnt the wrong instrument, the wrong combination of steps, a completely wrong choreography, he said. Two years with the same frayed trouser cuffs on the street in Dortmund. We hoped for some encouragement. No encouragement. We hoped for an answer. No answer. No letters. Nothing. Wuppertal, what squalor! he said. For two years you say nothing, two years. Two years in a row and not a word. Do you remember? Suddenly you say the word HEAD. Total eclipse. *The catastrophe will come*, you say, over and over again, *the catastrophe will come*, incessantly, *the catastrophe must come*. Do you remember? Love affairs, but non-impatient ones, over and done with in a flash, nothing. First your shoes come apart at the seams, then your head comes apart at the seams, breaks up in fits in starts. Your head breaks apart in fits and starts. At first you hear nothing as your head is breaking apart, he said, in fits and starts your head is breaking apart; you don't hear it. Insomnia and nausea alternate. Various pointless journeys, purposeless petitions, several escape attempts. To return was out of the question. Gomagoi was out of the question. Unwarrantedness, he said. Do you remember? Your talent as a speaker, my political phthisis, your fanaticism, my political uselessness. Do you remember? Several times he now said: do you remember? The emergence of revolutionary machinations. Our difference of opinion. Then we withdrew into the Maurachers' villa near Schruns with nothing but newspapers, from that point onwards nothing but newspapers.

From that point onwards everything came only from the newspapers, one's entire life, everything from that point onwards came
only from newspapers, each and every day heaps of newspapers.
Do you remember? Suddenly you remember your date of birth
again. Cultivation. *Occultation*, do you understand, he said. If
only we didn't have perfect pitch! he said. Every day I say to
myself, I have perfect pitch, every day, I have perfect pitch, I
have perfect pitch, I have perfect pitch! My feats of acrobatic artistry are nothing but feats of musical composition. Music. But
then too: our perfect pitch has *killed* us. Then the hairpin bend
in the road at *Unter*thurn, not *Ober*thurn, not, as with our parents, the hairpin bend in the road at *Ober*thurn, but rather the
hairpin bend in the road at *Unter*thurn. First it is the broken-up
instrument, said my brother, then it is the broken-up head. Do
you remember? If only we didn't have so much patience! I often
said that: if only we didn't have so much patience! And this high
art of saying that, he said. Do you remember? Anxiety about
burglars, about newspapers, gatherings of people. Having to
drown, to fall to the ground. When I was leading you by the
hand across the Suldenbach, I said, your uninterrupted weariness
of life. In your entire body. Uninterruptedly writing the word
anachronism on white paper, the word *conspiracy*. Do you
remember? Writing the sentence: *we like walking up to the Ortler
with our parents* a thousand times on white paper. Do you
remember? The word *obedient* two thousand times. Because we
dreaded human beings, there were so many human beings.
Because we dreaded our parents, we were always together with
our parents. Because we loathed the cities, we went into the cities.
Because we loathed the Ortler, we went up to the Ortler. Because

I loathed feats of acrobatic artistry, I studied feats of acrobatic artistry; because you loathed science, you studied science. The science of atmospheric strata, he said, because you hate everything having to do with atmospheric strata. Written matter, he said. Eventually fatigue, nothing but fatigue and anxiety about timetabled trains. Intellectual anxiety. And extreme mercilessness, extreme mercilessness. All of a sudden nothing but cold water, the cause of your back pains. Your cramped legs in bed, he said, your convulsively cramped legs. *If my existence outlasts my interest in my existence, for the remainder of it I shall be as good as dead.* Time and again: a letter! No, no letter! A letter! No, no letter! Do you remember? Outer restfulness, inner restlessness, never any inner restfulness. In identical garments even after the deaths of our parents, because we always loathed that, in our identical black trousers, identical black coats, with our identical black hats on our heads. In our *slouch*-hats, he said. And always in identical shoes. When I am thinking about my feat of acrobatic artistry, not a thought about food. When you are engaged in your scholarly work, not a thought about food. Then, at the Laganda Inn: inhaling nature, suddenly again inhaling nature in deep breaths and exhaling science, exhaling everything, everything. Exhaling garbage. Time and again all incidents were classic incidents. Do you remember? Making life into a habit of dying with the passage of years and with the dependability of science during those years. Do you remember? Thought is death, he said, then: in our forlornness we believed we were obliged to walk among human beings, obliged to rehearse feats of acrobatic artistry, obliged to toil away at science. Proverbs springing from forlornness. Unsoundness of mind springing from forlornness. And springing from forlornness into forlornness time and again. Simplification springing from a surfeit of complication, complication springing from a surfeit of simplification. Refinement because we loathe brutalization; brutalization because we loathe refinement. *Exactitude*, he said. Naturally an incessant suspicion of madness, he said. Through their method of simplification, they believed they were getting closer to us, but no such luck! Thanks to that method, thanks to everything else, they were distancing themselves more and more from us over the years; *we* of course had not withdrawn from them, he said, *we* hadn't done that, *they* distanced themselves from us; there is a difference; that is the thing that they are now accusing us of doing. But we shan't surrender ourselves ever again; we shan't afford any further occasions for the surrender of our body, our mind, our existence. We shan't let them get any closer to us again. Life as a habit, vigilance as a habit, nothing further. In truth my feats of acrobatic artistry killed me off a very long time ago, just as your scholarly work (on atmospheric strata) killed you off a very long time ago, said my brother. *One* of those feats of acrobatic artistry, the most difficult one, he said. *One* of your scientific points, who knows which. Because on account of one's interest in feats of acrobatic artistry, one cannot stop rehearsing them, he said. Because one cannot sever one's ties with them. It is the most perfect of all feats that has killed *me* off; it is the most concentrated of all thoughts that has killed *you* off, he said, The feat of acrobatic artistry is alive; the person who is rehearsing it is dead, he said. You are acquainted with his manner of speaking and so I need not draw your attention to its peculiarities. And you are familiar with my manner of speaking; in other words, with the way in which I listen. Since I have got used to my brother's way of speaking, because I have got used to my brother's illness, because I am familiar with his illness down to its most inconspicuous particulars. And as you know, all my life I have been concentrated on my brother's illness, I have for the most part, over the longest stretches of my existence, devoted myself to contemplating my brother's illness; I have kept everything pertaining to me in the background and have always kept everything pertaining to him in the foreground. Everything has only ever sprung from our cohabitation, nothing from me, nothing through me, everything from us, through us. Probably my brother will make no further appearances; my wish is for him to make no further appearances, to stay in Gomagoi. All signs point to his making no further appearances; probably recently, in the absence of any remarks to this effect from me, you have managed to ascertain that my brother's performances of his feats of acrobatic artistry have declined in quality; his feats have indeed long since ceased to be the perfect feats of acrobatic artistry that he used to exhibit. They have long since ceased to be the feats of acrobatic artistry that flabbergasted us. His feats of acrobatic artistry are not substandard, but they are no longer feats of acrobatic artistry that are perfect. He has found it impossible to perform a perfect feat of acrobatic artistry for quite a long time indeed; the progression of his illness, I think; doubts, and not only regarding his art, you cannot help thinking. And the impossibility of his continuing this colossal exertion that we are accustomed to from him. For such a long time my brother made the most demanding effort imaginable, a much more demanding effort than ever could have been required by his art, but now his effort has declined in intensity. He is not giving up, I think, but his art has declined in quality. And so it is my wish that in his own interest, as well as mine, as well as yours, as well as the general public's, he should make no further appearances, that for a certain period of time, and I am not thinking two or three years, we, he, should quite simply stay in Gomagoi; why in Gomagoi and not at the chalet in the Scheibenboden I shall explain later. Our ascent then decelerated appreciably. In point of fact, we were obviously not mastering the economy of ascents like the one to the Scheibenboden, which required the highest and most painstaking degree of economy. We were not fit for ascents like the one to the Ortler, like the one to the Scheibenboden, like any sort of venture involving an ascent from the Suldental. Our footfalls decelerated, which was probably also the cause of our conversation that was no conversation. But it was never sentimental, I must say, even if it had the semblance of sentimentality; we differed from all our acquaintances of a similar character and a similar age in that we disapproved of sentimentality, but it sometimes seems that what we used to find sentimental isn't sentimental after all, that it wasn't sentimental after all. The word *childhood*, like other words that always date from a very long time ago, gives rise to this notion. What a vast amount of landscape! What a vast amount of mental pathology! he suddenly said. When I think it is enough, landscape comes to light again. That is what is so frightening, the fact that landscape keeps coming to light again. Again: what a vast amount of landscape! Then: there is no use in maintaining that one is dead. *Onward! Onward!* he said in our father's tone of voice. And: *Higher! Higher!* in our father's tone of voice. You are aware of his proficiency in the art of mimicking voices. Near the Laganda Inn he said: but we shan't go to the Laganda, not to the Laganda. Too many memories, he said. Why feats of acrobatic artistry? he suddenly asked. Why feats of acrobatic artistry?

No question, he said. At first it's enough to stick out your tongue, he said. To rehearse a headstand. All of a sudden it's no longer enough to stick out your tongue and to rehearse a headstand. Unremitting work by the mind and unremitting work by the body, he said. This problem is what is so frightening. The cap donned askew is no longer enough, the left shoe on the right foot, and complementarily the right shoe on the left foot, are no longer enough. Doubt. Unbearability. A *different* feat of acrobatic artistry, *a more complicated* feat of acrobatic artistry, he said. The problem is that it's always the same and yet always a different feat of acrobatic artistry, always the same and yet always a different scholarly work. With refinement comes the refinement of despair, he said. Unfulfillable demands. Unfulfillable contracts. The difficulty consists in seeing more and more in the ever-more-eclipsing darkness, in seeing better, in seeing more, in seeing everything. In not perceiving unbearable pain as unbearable pain. In not perceiving snubs as snubs. In not going to the Laganda, he said, because he believed I wanted to go to the Laganda; in point of fact, we always used to go to the Laganda with our parents; but we were presuming that the Laganda had not changed in the intervening two or three decades. *Higher! Higher!* said my brother, you know his voice, you know the manner and fashion in which he speaks. In not perceiving the thinning air as ever-thinning air, even though the air is thinning, he said. The method is conceivably simple: everything is different. And if we turn up our collars, he suddenly said, the backs of our heads won't keep getting so cold. But we did not feel cold at all; to the contrary, both of us felt quite warm thanks to the rapidity of our ascent. No membership. Nothing. No church. Nothing, he said. But seclusion for too long, he suddenly said, is lethal. Being away from human beings for too long is lethal, he said. The chalet is lethal, he said. Practise drill after practise drill, nothing but practise drills. As we were crossing the Rosimbach, he said: at this spot I didn't want to go any farther. Do you remember? We were both exhausted. Waterlogged shoes, waterlogged feet, a condition of total exhaustion. Our anxiety in anticipation of the Scheibenboden, he said, do you remember? But our parents were merciless in the extreme. No lies, he said, no lies, no consideration. *Onward! Onward!* he said in our father's tone of voice; then *onward! Onward!* in the tone of voice of our mother. *Onward, boys! Onward!* Do you hear? he said, our parents are ordering us, ordering us to death once again. How we dreaded not being able to go any farther, he said. Do you remember? We went farther out of anxiety in anticipation of punishment. *Onward to the boulders*! they ordered. Our father would turn around and monitor us. We knew what it meant to lag more than a hundred paces behind our father. The three-day confinement. Do you remember? said my brother. The headpieces. Do you remember? We were well acquainted with everything near Razoi, the tree, the brook, everything. Even amid altered atmospheric conditions and hence altered soil conditions, my dear sir, more and more particulars that we were acquainted with, unobtrusive objects, roots, rocks, were unchanged. And along with these objects, along with this network of roots, with these rocks, there were the attendant threats of castigation from our parents. Obedience, said my brother. When we were walking through Gampenhofen, there was already anxiety in anticipation of sudden faintness, a dread of castigation. Our attacks of faintness, he said, beneath the Ortler, mental injuries as a consequence of the ascent of the Ortler. Our father, a practised mountaineer, was ruthless, infatuated with the mountains. Our mother was submissive. But back then there were already feats of acrobatic artistry, tricks. Going through the Suldental signified something worse than oppression. Your high walking speed, he said, and our decrepitude. Do you remember? And going up ever-higher mountains, up to ever-more unapproachable summits. Do you remember? *It is all a question of drawing the appropriate breaths,* said our father. Marching on and marching up and marching off into exhaustion. Our loathing of rucksacks and of everything *in* our rucksacks. Our loathing of mountain boots, he said. We loathe rucksacks and are walking to the Scheibenboden with rucksacks, he said. We loathe the Ortler and are walking to the Ortler. We loathe what we are doing, he said. The reason for our suddenly walking to the Ortler, and at the gloomiest time of year at that, was suddenly again *un*clear to us. Our parents had bequeathed to us the chalet on the Scheibenboden, but out of loathing of the Ortler and of the Scheibenboden and out of loathing of the chalet and out of loathing of everything having to do with the Ortler and with the Scheibenboden and with the chalet, we had not gone through the Suldental in over two decades, if not a full three decades, and because we had been in the world for decades, we had not been back to Gomagoi, we had stopped thinking about the chalet altogether, we had not gone back up to the Scheibenboden and the chalet. And now we were climbing to the Scheibenboden. For a reason *that appeared ever-more doubtful even to us as* all of a sudden, when we reached the end of the Suldental, the reason for our going up to the Scheibenboden became doubtful. But we did not talk about this. We climbed higher and higher and did not talk about it. We thought, we doubted, but we did not give voice to the fact that we were in doubt. We must have both have been thinking: suddenly we had, down in Gomagoi, where out of exhaustion by our, as you know, two very different professions, we were planning to stay at the Martell Inn for only *a couple of days; only a couple of days, then we'll go back again, only a couple of days, then we'll leave Gomagoi again*; in point of fact, my dear sir, two days earlier we still believed we were only going to be in Gomagoi for a couple of days; then suddenly: *a fairly good long while at the Scheibenboden, two, three years in the chalet*, even as all of a sudden everything was once again being cast into doubt, and so, my dear sir, the evening before we believed in the durability of our resolution, our resolution to go and spend two, three years in the chalet on the Scheibenboden, everything was so suddenly different; as recently as the evening before we had suddenly gotten the idea of hiking through the Suldental first thing next morning and then heading uphill, up to the chalet in order to inspect the chalet in the light of our intention of staying up on the Scheibenboden for two, three years; we had suddenly been smitten with this idea; both of us and not, as you will be thinking, my brother alone, had been smitten with it; we had been unable to sleep and had been thinking of nothing but the Ortler, which we could not get out of our heads, and that sudden flash of an idea in the evening was followed by the ascent in the early morning, a more than doubtful schema, you will be thinking, and how ridiculous must this seem to you, this account that you will possibly receive as soon as the day after tomorrow's mail delivery, but the truth is as follows: after walking from one end of Gomagoi to the other and back for several hours, we suddenly got the impression that the chalet at the Scheibenboden beneath the Ortler could be useful for our purposes: *for a short time,* I repeated, *for two, three years* it could be useful. And then all of a sudden, two-thirds of the way up, doubts had occurred to us. But then all of a sudden we thought that these doubts were occasioned by our exhaustion from the ascent and we suddenly had *no doubts whatsoever* again. And we even climbed higher with much greater intensity. By then we had only a good hour still ahead of us. During this interval my brother said the following, which I am now recording if not verbatim then at least *virtually verbatim*: we aren't walking down to the Laganda (to the aforementioned inn) because we aren't thinking of walking down to the Laganda, just as we are not walking to Sulden because we are not thinking of walking to Sulden, or we think we are walking down to the Laganda and we are not walking down to the Laganda and think we are walking to Sulden, etc. and are not walking to Sulden; we are not saying we are walking down to the Laganda even though we think we are walking down to the Laganda, we are not saying we are walking to Sulden, etc.; we are listening; we think we are walking to Sulden; we know we are not walking down to the Laganda, because we know that we are not walking down to the Laganda, etc.; it is possible for us to walk down to the Laganda, just as it is possible for us to walk to Sulden, but we are not walking down to the Laganda, we are not walking to Sulden, etc. We think about our walking as we do about our thinking, while we are thinking we are walking down to the Laganda, we are not walking to Sulden, because it is our wish not to walk to Sulden, not to walk down to the Laganda, etc., even though we are not walking down to the Laganda and not walking to Sulden; at the same time, we are not going down to the Laganda, not walking to Sulden, etc.; while we are walking, while we are thinking, while we are thinking, we are not walking down to the Laganda, not walking to Sulden. We are walking with our legs and thinking with our heads while we are not walking to Sulden and not walking down to the Laganda, etc., if we suddenly no longer had heads, he said, and suddenly could no longer walk, because we no longer had legs, but we both still have our head, etc. If we redouble the exertion of our will, he said, redouble the exertion of our will once again and make the most extreme exertion of our will once again, etc. How I wished we were already on the Scheibenboden! in the chalet!, my dear sir. Then my brother said in the manner of speaking that is also familiar to you, but much more breathlessly: perhaps even under these circumstances, at this altitude, it is possible for us to increase our strides, to ensure that we will move forward more quickly, to increase our strides without first increasing our velocity, or increase our velocity without increasing our strides, etc. Either you increase your strides, he said and not your velocity, while I increase my velocity but not my strides, or vice versa or vice versa, to make sure we stay together, side by side, he said. The thing to consider, he said, is whether we should increase our strides first but not our velocity, or increase our velocity first but not our strides. Or whether both of us should increase our strides *simultaneously* or both of us increase our velocity *simultaneously* or both of us simultaneously increase our velocity *and* strides. From the moment at which it became clear to us: everything comes from the head!, ever-greater seclusion, ever-greater coldness. Do you remember?

he asked. I don't remember, I said. Always a different method, always different people, always different settings, always different conditions. Do you remember? I don't remember, I said. Playing truant from school. An aversion to history, he said. When the large-scale connections were clear to us and the individual object was not and the individual person was not and the individual object and the individual person were clear to us and the large-scale connections were not. Make no warmth out of the cold, he said. Redouble our intellectual exertions. Increase our strides and redouble our mental exertions. No affection, nothing. No questions, nothing. No papers, nothing. No sums of money, no contracts, nothing. And then: if we go even farther than until now, when we believe we have gone as far as it is possible to go and transform our exertions once again into the utmost extremity of exertion and again at least, as we have done so often before, induce a redoubling of our strength of will, a redoubling which we, as we know, understand to mean a redoubling of our immediate intellectual capacity and hence an immediate redoubling of the causative energies of our head etc., we can count on thereby going farther, etc. and therewith simultaneously inducing a redoubling of our strength of will, a redoubling which we, etc. Abilities that we recognized as abilities very early on, etc. without being obliged to exist uninterruptedly in the oppression of our abilities, etc. We are anxious only in anticipation of being anxious, etc., as a result of the fact that we are walking with an ever-greater exertion of our will and thinking with an ever-greater exertion of our will and are not asking ourselves why and how and where to in *reality* during the act of walking and are not asking ourselves *why* during the act of thinking, because we are simply walking and simply thinking, etc., walking and thinking, which, as we know, has become our habit over the course of our life, etc. Suddenly, my dear sir: the fact that we are anxious when standing before the void in our head and before the void in the landscape called forth by the void in our head, before the over-sensitivity of our head, the fact that we do not know what it is that makes us think and what it is that makes us walk, do not know whether we should increase the velocity of our walking and of our thinking or decelerate them, discontinue them, he said. Suddenly he said *discontinue, discontinue, discontinue* several times. Because we do not know *how*, when we are walking, we are thinking about walking, *how*, when we are thinking, we are thinking about thinking, how, when we are thinking, we are thinking about walking, etc.; how we know nothing whatsoever about the mastery of our art. But we dare not speak of that. Thereafter, my dear sir, there was nothing. We were now at the site of the chalet, but of the chalet nothing was left but a shapeless heap of stones. Not even the skeleton of a building to protect us from the elements, nothing. Stones and beneath the stones the chalet's foundation. Everything had collapsed into rubble, everything. I erected a makeshift shelter for us out of stones and fragments of timber, because I did not want us to perish from exposure. We were too exhausted to climb back down that very day, but the next day we managed to reach the Suldental. At the Laganda Inn I was able to find a bed for my brother to rest in while I walked, as I was obliged to do, first to Sulden and then to Gomagoi to fetch help. Since this morning my brother has been residing in the Innsbruck suburb of Büchsenhausen, in an institution. I do not believe he will ever again make any appearances.

AT THE TIMBERLINE

It was as if the country were immersed in a profound musical cogitation.

Robert Walser

On the eleventh, late in the evening, a young woman and a young man, both from Mürzzuschlag as it transpired, got a room here at the inn. The two of them had already appeared in the common room to have something for supper shortly after their arrival. They ordered their food very quickly, and not in the least awkwardly, each of them acting on his or her own behalf and completely independently of the other all the while; I saw that they had been benumbed by the cold and were trying to get warm near the stove now. They said they were surprised at the overwhelming dearth of human beings here and asked how high above sea level Mühlbach was situated. The landlady's daughter stated that we were more than a thousand metres above sea level, which is not true, but I did not say 'nine hundred eighty'; I said *nothing*, because I did not wish to be distracted from my observation of the pair. Upon entering the common room they initially had not noticed me; then, as I saw, they were startled by my presence; they nodded to me, but afterwards they did not look over at me again. I had just started writing a letter to my fiancée; it would be wiser, I wrote to her, for her to put up with living with her parents a little while longer, until I got properly settled in

Mühlbach; only after I had secured two rooms for us outside the
inn, 'in Tenneck if possible,' I wrote, should she come here. In
her most recent letter, aside from hurling accusations at her
unsympathetic parents, she had written to me that she was afraid
of Mühlbach, and I replied that her fear was groundless. That her
condition was becoming so pathological that she was now afraid
of *everything*. For once the child existed, I wrote, she would again
be able to see clearly that everything *was* all right. It would be
wrong, I wrote, to get married before the end of the year; I wrote:
'Next spring will be a good time for that. In any case,' I wrote,
'whatever point in time the child arrives will be an embarrassing
one for the people around us.' No, I thought, you can't write that;
everything you have written so far in this letter is something that
you cannot write, that you cannot get away with writing; and I
started again from scratch and specifically with a sentence in
which I reported on something pleasant, something that would
take her mind off our misfortune, namely, the pay rise I had a
good chance of receiving in August. The station in Mühlbach
was off the beaten track, I wrote, but I was thinking, for me and
for both of us Mühlbach is a penal sentence, a death sentence, and
I wrote: 'Everybody on the police force is subject to being transferred at the discretion of the district inspector. At first I thought
my transfer to Mühlbach would be first and foremost a catastrophe for me and for us both, but I don't think that any more.
The station has its advantages. The inspector and I are completely independent,' I wrote, and I thought: a death sentence,
and I thought about what I would have to do in order to get out
of Mühlbach some day and descend back into the valley and
hence into the world of human beings, into civilization. 'If

nothing else, there are three inns in Mühlbach,' I wrote, but that's a foolish thing to write, I thought, and I crossed out the sentence, tried to make it illegible, and finally decided to write the whole letter anew a third time. (Lately I have been writing all my letters three, four, or even five times over, always in defiance of the agitation I feel while writing letters, which even affects my handwriting as well as my thoughts.) I was in the midst of writing that the police force was a good foundation for both of us, writing about my pay rise, about a weapons-training course that I would have to complete in Wels in the autumn, when the pair, the girl first, strangely enough, and the young man behind her, walked into the common room; writing that the inspector's wife had ailing lungs and was doomed and came from Celije in Slovenia. I continued writing, but I felt that I would not be able to mail this letter either; the two young people absorbed my attention from the very first instant; I perceived a sudden, complete inability on my part to concentrate on the letter to my bride-to-be; but I continued writing gibberish so that I could observe the two strangers better under the pretence that I was writing. I found it pleasant to see new faces for a change; because, as I now know, strangers never come to Mühlbach at that time of year, it was all the more remarkable to witness the unexpected appearance of the pair, of whom I presumed that he was a workman and she a student, and that both of them hailed from Carinthia. But then I noticed that the two of them were speaking a Styrian dialect. I recalled a visit to my Styrian cousin, who lives in Kapfenberg, and I knew both of them were from Styria; they talk that way there. It was not clear to me what sort of work the young man did; at first I thought he was a bricklayer, as was suggested by certain of his remarks, by words like 'joint mortar-binder', 'fire clay', etc.; then I thought he was an electrician; in fact he was a farmer. Gradually out of the pair's conversation there coalesced in my mind the image of an attractive household ('On a hillside,' I thought) that was still headed by the young man's sixty-five-year-old father. I learnt that the son regarded the opinions of his father, and the father the opinions of his son, as preposterous, that the father was feuding with his son and the son was feuding with his father. 'Stubbornness,' I thought. I pictured to myself a small town that the young man would have travelled to once a week for recreational purposes, a town where he would have regularly met up with the young woman there by the stove to whom he was now explaining his intentions regarding his father's property. He said he was going to compel his father to give it up, to abdicate. Suddenly the two of them laughed, only to fall completely silent for longer than they had been laughing.

The landlady brought them a copious amount of food and drink. As they were eating, much of their behaviour reminded me of our own. Just like that young man there, I have always had to do the talking while she keeps silent. Everything the young man said contained a threat. Threatening, it's all threatening. I hear that she is twenty-one (is he older?, younger?); that she has given up her studies (law!) That from time to time she becomes aware of the hopelessness of her situation and then takes refuge in reading scholarly (legal?) texts. That he is 'deteriorating', that more and more often she discerns what she calls 'applied brutality' in him. That he seems to be becoming more and more like his father, that this worries her. She talks of punches in the face dealt to brothers and cousins, of grievous bodily injuries, of indiscretions, of pitilessness on his part. Then she says, 'It was nice on the Wartbergkogel.' She says she likes his suit, and his new shirt as well. Their joint path to school ran through an alpine forest that they found terrifying; they recalled that an escaped inmate from the penitentiary in Göllersdorf in his prison uniform had tripped over a tree trunk and bled to death of a deep head wound, and that his body, which had been nibbled at by foxes, had been discovered by the two of them. They talked about a *premature birth* and about a money transfer . . . they had, I suddenly realized, already been away from Styria for four days; first they had been in Linz, then in Steyr, then in Wels. What could they be travelling with in the way of baggage, I thought. Apparently it's a lot of baggage, because the landlady had a hard time carrying it; I can still hear her; everybody can hear it when somebody is climbing up the stairs to the first floor and the guest rooms. The landlady went upstairs twice. By now, I thought, it will be warm in the room. What sort of room? In winter the main problem in country inns is keeping them warm. Wood-burning stoves, I thought. In the country in winter almost everything, I thought, is concentrated on keeping the buildings warm. I saw that the young man had on sturdy boots whereas the girl had on thin, low-sided shoes suitable only for city wear. On the whole, I thought, the girl is dressed completely inappropriately for this area and this time of year. Possibly, I thought, the two of them had absolutely no plans to stay in the country. Why Mühlbach? Who goes to Mühlbach who isn't forced to go there? After that, on the one hand I listened to what they were saying to each other after they had finished their meal but were still drinking beer, and on the other hand I read through what I had been writing all the while, and I thought, this is a completely useless letter, a thoughtless, vulgar, foolish, error-ridden letter. I can't get away with writing like this, I thought, not like this, and I thought I would sleep on it that night, that the next day I would write another letter. Being alone in a place like Mühlbach, I thought, ruins one's nerves. Am I ill? Am I crazy? No, I am not ill and I am not crazy. I was tired, but at the same time on account of the two young people I was incapable of leaving the common room and going up to the first floor, to my room. I told myself, it's already eleven o'clock, go to bed, but I did not go. I ordered myself another glass of beer and remained seated and scribbled ornaments, faces, on the stationery, the same unvarying faces that I have been scribbling on my writing paper out of boredom or veiled curiosity ever since I was a child. If only I could experience a sudden moment of clarity about these two young people, these lovers, I thought.

I chatted with the landlady as I eavesdropped on the two young people; I heard everything, and I suddenly got the idea that two of them were *in violation of the law*. I knew nothing more than that it definitely was not normal to do as these two had done, to arrive in Mühlbach late at night on the mail bus and to get a room, and in a moment of genuinely instantaneous insight I thought, the landlady is permitting them to spend the night together in a single room like a married couple, and I find this quite natural and I am behaving passively, observing; I am curious, I am sympathetic; I am not thinking this is something that undoubtedly calls for an intervention. An intervention? All of a sudden I start to toy with the idea of criminality in connection with the pair, as the young man in a loud voice, in an imperious tone, asks to settle up, and the landlady goes up to them and totals the bill, and when the young man opens his wallet I see that it has a great deal of money in it. No matter how close a watch their parents keep on them, I think to myself, every now and then these farmers' sons withdraw a fairly large sum from a bank account at their disposal and, taking a girl along with them, they go on a spending spree. The landlady asks when the two of them wish to be woken up in the morning and the young man says, 'at eight,' and now he looks over at me and puts a tip for the land-lady's daughter on the table. It is half-past eleven by the time the two of them have left the common room. The landlady clears away the glasses and washes them and then, rather than leaving at once, sits down next to me. I ask her whether the pair seem suspicious to her. Suspicious? 'Naturally,' she gives me to under-stand. Once again she tries to get closer to me in the coarsest manner imaginable, but I shove her away by prodding her chest with my flashlight, I stand up and go to my room.

Upstairs everything is quiet; I hear nothing. I know which room the two of them are in, but I hear nothing. As I am taking off my boots I think, I just heard a noise, yes, there was a noise. I actually listen out for a fairly long time, but I hear nothing.

Early in the morning, at six o'clock, I think to myself, I have slept only four hours, and yet I feel more refreshed than I usually do when I sleep, and downstairs in the common room I immedi-ately ask the landlady, who is scrubbing the floor, what the pair are up to. I added that they had preoccupied me all night long. He, the young man, said the landlady, had already risen at four

and left the house; she added that she did not know where he had
gone, that the girl was still up in his room. The pair have no baggage at all, the landlady now says. No baggage? Then what was
she, the landlady, lugging up into their room so laboriously yesterday evening? 'Firewood.' Of course, firewood. Now, ever
since the young man ran away at four in the morning ('I woke
up and I saw him,' says the landlady, 'goin' out into the cold without a coat . . . '), she has had a 'spooky' feeling about the two of
them. Had she demanded to see their passports, their identification cards, I asked. No, she hadn't asked to see any passports, any
identification cards. That's prosecutable, I said, but I said it in a
tone that never leads to anything. I ate my breakfast, but all the
while I was thinking about the two strangers, and the landlady
was also thinking about them, as I managed to observe, and
throughout the morning, which I spent at the station with the
inspector, and during which I was not allowed to leave the station
a single time, I was preoccupied with the two strangers. Why I
didn't say anything about the pair to the inspector is a question
I can't answer. In fact, I thought that it was only a matter of very
little time (of hours?) before it ended and that it was high time
for somebody to intervene. Intervene? How *and on what grounds*
could anybody intervene? Should I report the incident to the
inspector, or should I not report it to him? A pair of lovers in
Mühlbach! I laughed. Then I fell silent and did my work. My
task was to put together a new list of residents. The inspector is
trying hard to get his wife transferred from the Grabenhof tuber-
culosis sanatorium to the one in Grimmen. He said this transfer
was costing him a great deal of petitionary effort, a great deal of
money. But, he added, in Grabenhof her condition was deteriorating; he said that there was a better doctor in Grimmen. That

he was going to have to take a whole day off and travel to
Grabenhof and take his wife to Grimmen. That the twenty years
that he and his wife had lived in Mühlbach had been enough to
make her, a native of the town of Hallein, terminally ill. 'Now
of course a normal person won't come down with a lung condition in this clear air, up here in the mountains,' said the inspector.
I have never seen the inspector's wife because as long as I have
been in Mühlbach she has never been back home. She has been
in the Grabenhof sanatorium for five years. He asked me how
my bride-to-be was faring. He knows her, he even danced with
her the last time she was in Mühlbach; the fat old man, I think,
gazing at him. It was 'madness' to get married too early, and it
was very much also 'madness' to get married too late, he said. In
the second half of the morning he allowed me to write my letter
('write,' he ordered) to my fiancée at last. All of a sudden I had
a clear head for the letter. That is a good letter, I said to myself
once I had finished it, and it doesn't contain even the smallest of
white lies. I would send it off immediately, I said, and walked
over to the mail bus, which had already finished warming up and
drove off as soon as I had given the driver my letter; on that day
it did not have a single person in it apart from the driver. It was
twenty-one degrees below zero, I noted on checking the ther-
mometer just beside the front door of the inn as the landlady,
standing in the open passageway, beckoned me inside. She said
she had been knocking over and over again for hours at the door
of the room the girl was sleeping in and received no answer,
'nothing.' I immediately went up to the first floor and to the door
of the room and knocked. Nothing. I knocked once again and
said that the girl had to open the door. 'Open up! Open up!' I
said several times. Nothing. As there was no spare key to the

room, the door would have to be forced open, I said. The land-lady silently assented to my forcing open the door. I needed only to thrust my upper body forcefully against the door frame one time and the door was open. The girl was lying diagonally on the double bed, unconscious. I sent the landlady to the inspector. I noted that the girl had been seriously poisoned by drugs, and I covered her with the winter coat that I had taken down from the window grate; obviously the winter coat was the young man's. Where is he? Without saying a word everybody was asking him-self where the young man was. I thought that the girl had attempted suicide only *after* the disappearance of the young man (her fiancé?). The floor was strewn with pills. The inspector was nonplussed. Now we would have to wait until the doctor arrived, and we all saw once again how difficult it is to get a doctor to come up to Mühlbach. It might be an hour before the doctor shows up, said the inspector. Two hours. You never want to find yourself needing a doctor in Mühlbach, he said. Names, dates, I thought, dates, and I searched the girl's handbag, to no avail. In the coat, I thought, and I searched the coat that I had covered the girl with; I was looking for a wallet. As it turned out, the young man's wallet was indeed in the coat. His passport was also in the coat. WÖLSER, ALOIS, BORN 1.27.1939 IN RETTE-NEGG, RETTENEGG BEI MÜRZZUSCHLAG, I read. Where is this man? This fiancé of hers? I dashed downstairs to the common room and used the phone to notify all stations of the incident, which seemed to me to justify the issuing of a war-rant for the arrest of Wölser. The doctor will have to get here right away, I thought, and when he arrived a half an hour later, it was too late: the girl was dead.

That simplifies everything now, I thought; the girl is staying in Mühlbach.

The landlady was very quick to have the corpse taken out of the inn and placed in the morgue across the street. There the girl lay, gaped at uninterruptedly by the inquisitive Mühlbachers, for two days, while her parents were being traced, and on the third day Mühlbach finally witnessed the arrival of *Mr and Mrs Wölser*, Wölser's parents, who were also the girl's parents; to everyone's horror it transpired that the young man and the girl were siblings. The girl was immediately transported to Mürzzuschlag; her parents accompanied her in the hearse. As of then her brother and their son remained nowhere to be found.

Yesterday, the twenty-eighth, two lumbermen surprisingly found him frozen to death just below the timberline above Mühlbach, and lying under two hefty chamois that he had killed.

MIDLAND AT STILFS

Outsiders, people not in on the secret of our upbringing, may regard our demeanour, when the Englishman is here, as an insane demeanour; they may regard us ourselves, our atmosphere at Stilfs, as an artificial, insufferable atmosphere. Even though we exist in perpetual fear of our friend suddenly visiting us, even though throughout the year we dread his suddenly turning up at Stilfs in the blink of an eye, we are simultaneously also always thinking: if only our friend would suddenly turn up, that would really be something!, for all of us find nothing more terrifying, find nothing more and more menacing, especially at the end of winter, than to be here at Stilfs, in the highlands, or rather, in the mountains, which reign supreme here as manifestations of absolute nature, over long, indeed the longest stretches of time, to be here alone, dependent entirely on ourselves, without a single interloper, a single foreigner. We dread visitors, indeed we loathe them, and at the same time we cling to the outside world with all the despair of those who are cut off from it. Our destiny's name is Stilfs, everlasting solitude. In truth, we can count on our own fingers the people who visit us every now and then as so-called desired persons, but we are afraid of being visited even by these so-called desired persons, because we are afraid of all people who might visit us; we have developed a colossal fear of them even though there is nothing we await with more eagerness than some other human being—and how often we think: it doesn't matter what sort of human being, let him be an *in*human being for all we care!—visiting us and interrupting our montane martyrdom, our lifelong spiritual exercitation, our solitudinous inferno. We have resigned ourselves to existing on our own, and yet we keep thinking somebody could come to Stilfs, and when somebody does visit us, we don't know if it is senseless or deleterious, or deleterious *and* senseless, for this person to visit us; we ask ourselves whether it is *necessary* for this person to come up here to Stilfs; whether it is not an ignoble violation of our code of solitude or our salvation. In point of fact, we perceive most of the people who still come up here, the few who still dare to venture up to us at all—for confirmed facts and unconfirmed rumours sap their resolve, render them incapable of forthrightly seeking out Stilfs—as deleterious pests. Once such a person is gone again, we spend days contemplating the degree of destruction he has wrought in us. We then say nothing and attempt via our silence and doubled and tripled manual labour in the stables and on the threshing floors and in the woods first to tolerate and then to palliate and nullify the paralysis that this visitor has wrought in us. We become horrifyingly conscious of what a colossal punishment Stilfs is for us when, after having suddenly been assaulted by one of these surprise visitors in the shortest time and with the utmost force, we intensify our attention to our domestic chores, work one another to exhaustion in an exaggerated access of manual labour. The truth is this: that this thing which we wish to escape from but which is imprisoning us with ever-greater ruth-lessness has grown into an insuperable permanent condition, that this thing, Stilfs, which we of course love out of habit, but also for rational reasons abhor with the utmost profundity, indeed loathe with a downright humiliating obsessiveness; that this thing, Stilfs, is something sought out by these people whom we have known from our earliest, early, and later childhood and post-childhood, from the most various holiday resorts and places of study, who seek Stilfs out for the most various purposes, for the purpose of recreation or defamation or annihilation. These people are all unrelated to us; our relatives no longer come here. And in the future they won't either, and even if they do it will only be reluctantly for the purpose of dying or claiming a legacy. The people who still visit us are not related to us, and we inter-rogate each other about our shared acquaintances. All these people are nothing but inquisitiveness personified, and the majority of them talk loudly and misuse everything, and yet, we think, it's good for a change to have different turns of phrase from our own, different thoughts from our own, at Stilfs; then we think, this person has still done us wrong; we have been trai-tors to ourselves for days, for weeks; why didn't we throw this person over the wall within the very first hour, etc. To us the visitors who come up here signify a waste of time and hence sig-nify misfortune. There are, however, some of them, the fewest of the few, the rarest of the rare, who make us happy. The Englishman is such a visitor. But even he, when he is here, says what Stilfs is, says that we have no idea of what it is, that we do not acknowledge what it is, that we loathe Stilfs, that we inces-santly defame Stilfs in the most criminally slanderous fashion, etc., that he cannot come to terms with the notion, and why should he?, that for us Stilfs is satiety, apathy, despair. *Repose* and *the possibility of concentration*, he says; these are words that we have heard time and again, that are familiar to all of us, who know that Stilfs is the opposite of them. What is more, all these people commit the felony of garrulity, of telling us incessantly, at every opportunity, what Stilfs really is, what we don't realize that it is, these people who live on stupidly trustful terms with the whole world the whole year round and satisfy all their needs in the big cities. Like some imbecile of a layman flush with all the brazenness of the present age and with unbridled arrogance trying to explain to a craftsman his own craft: thus do our visitors try to explain Stilfs to us. Everything that comes out of their constantly open mouths says that they know what we do not know. They incessantly reply to questions regarding Stilfs that in their opinion we have no less incessantly posed, even though we have never posed a single question regarding Stilfs to our visitors. Because we know everything about Stilfs. Our visitors' opinions regarding Stilfs are of no interest to us, because we have been acquainted with it for decades. But even the Englishman, who all told has spent no more than fourteen days and nights at Stilfs, explains Stilfs to us. As we were walking away from the grave of his sister, who exactly fifteen years ago today plunged headfirst from the high wall into the Alz to her death, he, Midland, said that he had become conscious that we—and he meant not only Franz and me but also Olga and Roth, all of us—were existing in the most ideal locale imaginable. That he could not imagine a more ideal locale for us. That indeed, he suspected us of deliberately keeping silent about the fact that here at Stilfs we were developing in ideal conditions, that we had probably been, as he put it, jointly or separately accomplishing scientific work that, in being commensurate with our clear minds, was of enormous value. He was joking, of course; he said 'epoch-making intellectual produce', but he meant what he said, in all seriousness. He said that when he was here at Stilfs, when he was walking across the courtyard, when he was inhaling and taking into consideration everything subsumed under the concept of *Stilfs*, he got a sense of the colossal dimensions of the material that we, Franz and I, had already worked up into a science that had been an indispensably precious contribution to knowledge for the longest time, a science that in reality we ourselves have not given a thought to in a very long time indeed. He supposes that we had completed a book-length work of natural history but that for reasons he cannot fathom we refused to publish it. That we entrenched ourselves behind our fear of the world in the most senseless fashion. He said that what was no longer possible outside Stilfs for him, for anybody, was possible here. That he had proofs of our development, that everything about us was proof that we were as advanced as we could only dream of being. That he felt like a laggard in our company at Stilfs. That everything he had done so far was still stalled at its rudimentary stage. That all attempts to cope on his own with the inchoate rubbish in his brain had foundered on the shoals of his own nature and those of external nature. That the megalomania of a ruthlessly ratified external world had been a lifelong lethal misfortune for him. That in the big cities for the mere sake of not being inevitably suffocated by their feeblemindedness he had been compelled to expend, to squander, all his energies in society even as he had been unable to live at all outside it. ('The crowd wears you down to nothing!') We, though, had been saved, he said, saved at Stilfs; we had recognized Stilfs for what it was; in it, we had taken possession of the most felicitous of possessions. He said that for us here the future was an open road free of obstructions. That Franz was pursuing his journey, and I was pursuing mine. That at Stilfs everything concerning us was clear to him, *hyper*clear. And how untrue everything he says is; the reality is the opposite of what he thinks it is. *Minor difficulties*, he says, lest we should be frightened to death by him in our good fortune, and he spells out to us a list of all the merits of Stilfs, a succession of gruesome blemishes and a couple of ludicrous ones, but the minor difficulties and blemishes that he enumerates to us—thoughtlessly, we feel—are in reality the greatest ones imaginable, and Stilfs is, as I said, not any sort of ideal thing, but rather lethal to us. Our existence is a lethal existence. Stilfs is the end of life. But if I say what Stilfs is, I shall be taken for a madman. For the same reason Franz also refrains from saying what Stilfs is. And Olga is not asked and Roth is incapable of answering. Naturally we are all insane. But when a person is incessantly asserting something that is not only a hundred per cent untrue and omits no opportunity of adducing this assertion, when indeed at bottom and in reality he no longer exists on the basis of anything but this assertion, or in any case still exists solely on the basis of such an assertion, one's nerves are tested to their very limits. Stilfs! Of course I myself—just like Franz, as I know for a fact—regarded even my most elementary thoughts in an insane manner the moment I was sentenced in the coarsest and therefore most inexcusable manner to Stilfs and to the Stilfsian penal system in force here, and I immediately renounced those thoughts. To be sure, down in Basel, in Zurich, in Vienna, I, like Franz, still believed that at Stilfs—which even when living among all those people I always regarded as a quintessence of stillness and meditation, whereas in reality it has never been anything but a high-elevation hotbed of admittedly extraordinary dim-wittedness and dull-wittedness, a centre of *cultural dull-wittedness*—that at Stilfs I would be able to think what I could not think in Basel, in Zurich, in Vienna, and finally in that thoroughly intellectually malnourished town of Innsbruck; that at Stilfs what was impossible for me (and Franz) in all those university towns would be possible, namely, to develop in a manner commensurate with my utterly auspicious intellectual abilities, just as Franz believed that he could save himself from inconsequentiality as a student down below by diving headlong into this Stilfs that was waiting for us up here, that frightfulness would be turned into fruitfulness, imprecision into precision, unclarity into clarity on this estate situated high up in the trust-inspiring mountains, that mental oppression would be turned into mental elation, etc., but I was mistaken, and Franz was also mistaken: at Stilfs, nothing has issued from us but the pitifulness of two utter washouts. Down below we thought of amelioration. Up above radical deterioration had made its entrance. At night I often wake up and say to myself: at Stilfs you have annihilated yourself!, or: at Stilfs they have annihilated you! Stilfs is nothing but masonry, rock, the breath of balderdash. Stilfs is nothing. And the people come up here and tell us what Stilfs is. They come up here with their perverse intellectual short-circuit, like the Englishman, the son of wealthy parents, a fanatical admirer of mountains, who is pacing up and down the courtyard now, as I am observing him through my window. I can see him; he cannot not see me. 'Tackling real problems, transforming the world, at Stilfs!'—that is what I am hearing him saying. But we love the Englishman. He arrives and goes to his room and takes a bath and spends the whole evening talking about the ideas that he has (and that we do not have) and says that he believes in the actualization of these ideas, that it's all a matter of realizing them. He uses German as skilfully as English, uses both of them so well that one would think he had always spoken both of them. His German-English sentences are interspersed with French words subordinated to a rhythmic principle. He does not expect to be interrupted. He revels in his own art of formulation. He imparts a steady, unvarying intonation to his voice, as though as a matter of principle he were occasionally adding or withholding emphasis just where anyone else would do the opposite. The other person immediately thinks that he is a man who is inured to the most exacting demands. Franz is a source of metaphysics. It would appear, he says, that Midland has already turned into an entirely political mind. He says that *civilization* is infused with illness. That science does not yet know how to describe the illness. But that the illness is a terminal one. The highest velocities in his head. He speaks about writers in a tone of intellectual coldness. About philosophers in one of contempt. He says that he detests science as well as the Church. That nowadays the common people are also nothing but bellyaching dull-wittedness. That destruction is creation. This manic fanatic talks of clearing the old furniture out of all the nation-states. This is the same man who a couple of hours ago said that everything was unsurpassably disgusting now. What an incredible fascination this person exerts on me, I think, this person who is outfitted

in all the hallmarks of a world that we have known only by hear-
say for many years, a world that we, to be honest, no longer have
the faintest notion of, a world that, indeed, we would no longer
venture to return to at all if we were suddenly granted the possibility of returning to it, to the world, which has already become
completely incomprehensible to us and from out of which
Midland with his peculiar art of surprising has surfaced all of a
sudden, as if upon the outer shell of an adamantine mass of infin-
ity, at Stilfs, where there is no longer an out there or a down there
for us; I observe him as in a rapid series of gestures he—what a
young, good looking physique he has, I think—sketches a geo-
metrical figure on the floor of the courtyard, which has been dyed
a cold, artificial green hue by the morning sun, as he, a Briton to
the core, whose father studied with my father twenty-five years
ago at that London university that was then still struggling with
their insignificance; I observe how the Briton, apparently ever-
mindful of the effortlessness with which he is capable of outfitting
the mastery of his own body in ever-more-refined elegance, is
bridging the interval of time in which he is at Stilfs, the handful
of hours before he sets off again. It is, I think as I observe him,
his habit to take hold of the thoughts that preoccupy him using
words pertaining to these thoughts and spoken aloud from time
to time, a habit from which one may infer that the weight of all
his thoughts is precisely distributed in his brain. Although
throughout the evening he spoke on the most various topics,
rhapsodized, improvised, about a heap of news from England
and from all over Europe, I noticed that there was but a single
thing that interested him: how it would be possible for him to
misuse everything that his brain had been appropriating for
nearly three decades, and that had been accumulating in his brain

over the same period in the most decisive fashion, as the basis of a work that would be the product of his own entirely unique nature; for years he has been thinking of nothing but taking that body of thought that nature has built up into a colossal arsenal of ideas in his brain, and that has already become superfluous to him there, and additionally ratifying this body of thought in the eyes of the outside world, meaning the world outside his own mind, via the production of a work in black and white. It is not without significance that he, probably unbeknownst to himself, often utters the word *actualization*, and nearly everything he says is centred on the concept of *realization*. This is the same man who has made a tradition of visiting his sister's grave once a year. He himself says that he feels nothing at his sister's grave, that her face is no longer conceivable for him, that he has long since ceased to be able to picture his sister at all, that when he stands next to her grave, he feels nothing but the embarrassment felt by every grave visitor, that self-loathing, self-contempt wells up within him on these occasions. That the cult of the dead is unappetizing in the extreme, more repulsive than any other. But he says that it has probably been a very long time indeed since his annual visits to Stilfs ceased to have anything to do with his late sister, this dead woman who has long since ceased to be present to him in any sense and with whom he did not enjoy a particularly close relationship even during her lifetime. That his reason for coming here is not his sister but Stilfs, whereas it used to be not Stilfs but, rather, his late sister. That his sister, 'that nullity under the stone slab of that grave' (Midland), seemed a complete stranger to him during her lifetime; that he never loved her, let alone had any attachment to her; that suddenly once she was dead, after the accident—and even in connection with that he no longer recalls the death itself but only the circumstances that led up to it, the rocky ledge and so forth, the roar of the Alz—that suddenly after her death, he was harrowed by guilt. He said that as long as his sister had been *living beside him*, as he put it, he had paid her little mind, indeed, no mind whatsoever. That she had been a person quite devoid of substance for him, that she had always struck him as being an individual of absolutely no concern to him. That by now even this guilt had turned into a habit. It is not his sister that keeps him coming to Stilfs; it is Stilfs itself. He says that we are the reason. That he comes to Stilfs. That he is delighted. Midland, I think, who is always close enough to being in a good mood to get back into such a mood every time; unlike us, who no longer ever allow ourselves to be in a good mood, let alone to enjoy what he calls the lust for life. I have often seen the Englishman laughing and he is not at Stilfs but in England or somewhere even farther away from Stilfs, and I see him in my mind's eye, as I often do in moments of deep despair; I see him laughing. He says that his father was only 'a wise-cracker', his mother 'a wicked falsification of the miracle of nature'. The art of surprise. Not a trace of fatigue, even though he had just travelled from Nepal in the course of a single day; he was full of impressions of his travels, impressions with which he—a person incapable of retaining whatever is pent up inside him for more than an instant under any circumstances—regaled us immediately and ever-more pedantically until five in the morning. He often derives the most unalloyed enjoyment from all the things that we can never even find bearable. He reads books, newspapers, the oldest as well as the newest among them, with the greatest attentiveness, which is why he has such interesting things to talk about. He never tires of studying the incessantly changing world, and as he studies it, he criticizes it, multiplies it, divides it. He is an elucidator of general as well as particular intellectual insanity; he lines up one experience after another, and in the end in every case he sees nothing but lies, deceit, bottomlessness, infamy. He is extraordinarily well schooled in mistrustfulness. He says that he would not be an Englishman, a Midland, if everything did not have two sides for him, two sides of which one never knows which is the greater, the grosser, the baser, in its vileness. The Europeans, he says, are deeply mired in their own complexes, and they will never manage to extricate themselves from these complexes; their history is now definitively concluded. Revolution in Europe, he says, is mere mischief-making; by now it is merely indurating and obfuscating something that has been nothing but pure agony for centuries. But today, he says, it is not only Europe that is at its end, at the end that 'we are privileged to be living through'; the world itself is at its end. And yet at the same time, he says, this is opening up enormous possibilities, an extremity of concentration on outer space, on the immensities of the universe. The Englishman is not uninterruptedly coarsening his utterances like the others; in point of fact, in his total, transparent fearsomeness, he amplifies and illuminates everything he talks about; unlike the other people, he is not continually contracting the scope of his talk; he makes each of his topics into an infinitely expansive topic, whereas the other people's topics are always dwindling; in most conversations, as we know, the topic shrinks down to a puny scrap of conversational material, and very quickly to nothing. To and fro, to the well and back, the Englishman paces and waits for Franz or me to tell him that breakfast is ready, that he can come in. In observing him I get the impression that he is well rested, even though it was not until six in the morning that we retired to our rooms, where, I think, and as was proved by the chink of light under his door, he stayed up another hour reading a book. To think, I think, that after only two or three hours many young people can be completely well rested, can have gathered enough energy to normalize their minds and bodies, whereas we, Franz and I, not to mention Olga—and even Roth needs plenty of sleep—have to sleep six to seven hours, which means that we go to bed relatively early, which I find quite natural when I reflect on the fact that we have to keep running the farm as it always has been run, not to mention the correspondences that we have to carry on, the correspondences relating to the farm, the correspondences with all sorts of doctors regarding Olga, with the district and regional law courts regarding Roth. Originally, two hundred years ago, this farm was meant to be run by two or three dozen servants and labourers, but we run it in its original form on our own. And we run it with greater intensity than our predecessors, even though it is less profitable; indeed, every day it becomes clearer and clearer to us that agriculture, especially at such an altitude, is an absolutely pointless enterprise. Running a farm like this one is suicidal. For decades, and this is the truth, we have been overworked completely pointlessly; that is the really horrible thing. But there is nothing left for us to do but work ourselves to death here. What is more, we feel that the whole thing is ridiculous. At the end of each day, we are exhausted, and we have always been exhausted as long as we have been at Stilfs; at Stilfs, we have only ever existed in a single state of exhaustion. Our natural state is this state of exhaustion. Against our wills we exist in the extremity of exertion, which induces fatal exhaustion. The moment we were sentenced to imprisonment at Stilfs—sentenced by the dread powers that be, our parents—we thought, if we are going to have to spend the rest of our lives here at Stilfs, as we are already too weak even to think of escaping, we mustn't let Stilfs fall into ruin. And so Stilfs is now intact; its farming infrastructure is intact, but its residential buildings are not intact. In point of fact, the degree of neglect in the residential buildings is extreme, unimaginable. Whereas the farming infrastructure is now in better shape than it ever has been—because we have long since concentrated on nothing but the farm; the farm is the only reason we are still here; we have long since totally surrendered ourselves, by which I mean totally surrendered ourselves for the sake of the farm—the residential buildings are more dilapidated than any other such buildings I have ever seen. Everything about them makes a demoralizing impression, an extremely demoralizing impression; the floors and ceilings are sagging; specifically, they look as though they are sagging under the weight of the mice that are proliferating beneath and above them with incomparable ferocity; the walls and the furniture are the very picture of neglect, and the house is permeated by a foul stench that emanates from them, such that the vermin that are teeming in the billions now reign unchallenged everywhere; everything is dank and musty and you feel as though you are bound to suffocate. As for the furniture, that potentially highly valuable remnant of our ancestors' idyllic flight into the realm of taste: we have no ability to appreciate it. Every object in every room has been abandoned to the ravages of time for literally decades. For example: the upholstery of the wing chairs in our drawing room is now completely in tatters. In the cabinets and chests of drawers there are heaps of sawdust. Over the years, the paintings on our walls have fallen down of their own accord, and for the most part we have stopped even bothering to pick them up. After every tremor that erupts from the earth—and the earth trembles several times a year at Stilfs— the devastation gets a little worse. We no longer lay a finger on anything. We never pick anything up; we climb over it. It must be remembered that all our rooms are cluttered to the bursting point with baroque and Josephine antiques—there are tabernacle cabinets and secretary desks all over the place; I shudder to think of our mother's mania for the Empire—with tables and chairs, etc., etc., along with heaps of the kitschy bric-a-brac of child- hood. Over the briefest span of time, I think, everything here at Stilfs is being smashed to pieces; in no time at all, everything here will be permanently irreparable. If we seriously wished to con- serve, to safeguard, this thing that has kept us from breathing for decades and in the midst of which all of us have always believed ourselves bound to suffocate, this thing that is nevertheless basi- cally the most valuable thing at Stilfs, namely, its interior furnishings, its arty-crafty trinkets, the majority of which are three hundred, four hundred years old and hail from all sorts of countries, these hundreds of heirlooms made of the costliest noble woods, not a few of which heirlooms were conceived and constructed specifically for Stilfs over many years by craftsmen who must be termed artists; if we seriously wished, I say, to con- serve, to safeguard all this stuff we grew up in the midst of—and in the midst of a hopelessness that was initially blurry and then all of a sudden became as elementally clear as could be—two dozen people would have to be employed round the clock on this work alone, quite apart from the fact that the outbuildings like the hunting lodge, the greenhouses, etc., are also here, that they, too, are falling into decay literally day by day with even greater ingenuity, and will continue to do so until they have fallen entirely into decay; money would not be allowed to play any role whatsoever in this, even though it obviously plays the most important imaginable role in everything, and we ourselves would be required to apply our appreciation of all this stuff that over time has been ruined by time, even though in reality we have not the merest scintilla of appreciation of it. Everywhere, all these art objects on the floors and on the walls remind one of the fact that Olga, who loved all these things, has by now been confined to her invalid's chair for ten years and in reality is no longer present here at all. Olga reproaches Franz and me for our brutish and dim-witted disposition to these art objects. And in point of fact, we have found these furnishings of ours oppressive all our lives and we have loathed them. If everything is an anachronism nowadays, as the Englishman said yesterday, what a mighty anachronism must Stilfs be! It would be logical, it would be logically cogent, Franz asserted yesterday evening, for us to shuffle off at a second's notice, for us to kill ourselves without hesitation, because, as Franz asserts, the sole possible logically cogent option still left to us is to kill ourselves; it makes no difference how we do it, the quicker the better, but we are too weak to do it, we talk about it, and quite often we talk for hours, days, weeks on end about it and do not kill ourselves; to be sure, we think—to be sure, we know—how senseless it is for us to keep living, for us to keep existing, but we do not kill ourselves; we do not follow the examples of those who have already killed themselves, and quite a number of people our age have, as we know, already killed themselves, for all sorts of ridiculous reasons, for reasons that are incredibly ridiculous by comparison with our reasons; we do not kill ourselves and each day we grapple anew with every possible kind of pointlessness, we waste the day on pointless handicraft and the absurd dissipation of our memories, we plague ourselves and feed ourselves and terrify ourselves and do nothing else and that is precisely the most senseless thing in the entire world, the fact that we plague and feed and terrify ourselves, that is the most repellent thing of all, but we do not kill ourselves, we make the thought of suicide our only thought, but we do not commit suicide. We had already had our supper when the Englishman, who has just now stopped in the middle of the courtyard, suddenly, without knocking—the doors and gates had not yet been locked and bolted—turned up in the room giving onto the courtyard. Franz and I had just had a talk about Roth, who over supper had once again threatened to burn Stilfs to the ground. We had drawn the lad's attention to the fact that he— and here we pointed at him—could be locked up without further ado merely for having made this threat; he could be locked up for years, we said, and we added that it was up to him to decide whether he preferred to be locked up in the asylum or in the penitentiary, whereupon he calmed down and promised not to burn Stilfs to the ground. We are quite fond of the lad and need him; we provide him with the same food and drink that we provide ourselves with and at bottom he is better off at Stilfs than anywhere else, as nowhere else can keep a madman, especially a madman as burly as Roth is, better fed with such a minimum of fuss. If he were not at Stilfs, he would have long since been left to the company of convicts and lunatics. This place is the most important thing that he knows, and as long as he doesn't burn Stilfs to the ground and doesn't increase the average number of cows he keeps stabbing with the kitchen knife and doesn't increase the average number of chickens he keeps inflating with the bicycle pump until they explode, the fact that he is insane will make no difference to us. We are well aware that Roth is a problem, but we ourselves are a problem for ourselves and our problem is a bigger one. We have conferred about the fact that it is getting more and more difficult to curb Roth's excesses, that we cannot allow ourselves to forbid him his visits to the tavern— in the summer he swims across the Alz in his shirt and trousers and walks soaking wet all the way to the pub—that to the contrary, he must be allowed to go into the valley and across the Alz and into the pub *whenever he likes*, because however late at night he comes back, be it at three a.m. or even later, he is always completely pacified by then. If we did not have Roth, utter chaos would reign at Stilfs and Olga would have nobody to look after her, for in point of fact we, Franz and I, cannot be bothered to look after our sister; we forget about her most of the time, but Roth does her many favours in addition to providing her with the minimum necessities. He is a hard worker who, when he is instructed skilfully and with good humour, performs the toughest jobs, the most arduous jobs, the most thankless and unthinkable jobs, to our satisfaction. Because we work just as hard as Roth does and do not spare ourselves the most oppressive tasks, he has no dodges at his disposal. He respects us. His parents died young; his father hanged himself; two years ago, his only brother bet ten schillings that he could swim across the Mur when it was in flood, and because he actually dived into the Mur—the Roths are Styrians—he drowned; ever since then Roth has complained about not having anybody left in the place he comes from, namely, Styria. His best and only friend threw himself in front of a train in March. The Englishman lingeringly perused the obituary and the accompanying picture of the unfortunate man. Doomed to commit suicide, Roth's friend, an inmate at an asylum, had been released from the institution every weekend so that he could visit his parents; the last time instead of returning to the asylum he went to the railway embankment. The Englishman said that Roth's friend had flung himself in front of the train not a day earlier or later than 11 March, his birthday. Roth inherited the unfortunate man's clothes, including a pair of lederhosen whose legs go all the way down to his ankles. Now the only clothes Roth ever puts on are those of his dead friend; immediately upon the arrival of the Englishman, Roth had donned the suicide's Sunday best and gone down from Stilfs to the pub via the Alz. He had already taken his leave and the Englishman had given him a tip, a pound note, as he always does during his visits. He has always given Roth a pound note; then Roth had also rushed out to the stables and killed the three chickens that we are going to eat today; on Saturdays he kills the chickens that we eat on Sunday; he swings them in circles above his head with his arms outstretched and decapitates them. Already clad in his Sunday best, his sole Sunday outfit, he directed the Englishman's gaze to a point just below the door of the room giving onto the courtyard and said that the chicken was perfectly normal but for the fact that it was missing its head; he picked up this remark from Franz, who used to make this remark all the time, until he suddenly got sick of it, at which point Roth adopted it. I cannot help recalling previous visits by the Englishman—who now gives me the impression that he doesn't know whether he is supposed to wait for us in the courtyard or to come inside to see us; he is waiting for the invitation to come in for breakfast; nobody is calling him, Franz is not calling him; I am not calling him—I cannot help recalling Midland's previous visits as I stand at the window and observe him; it is possible, I think, that down in the valley, at the pub, friends of his are waiting for him and he wants to leave; it may even be the case that down on the bank of the Alz he left a young woman, a girlfriend, to spend the night on her own at the house of one of those poor people with rooms to let, for he only ever shows up here at Stilfs on his own, with nobody else; it would not be the first time people had stopped off at the tavern down below—two years ago a group of Swedish archaeologists, north Germans, Italians (he is friends with so many people from all sorts of countries) were waiting for him—while he was up here at Stilfs. On no account, he once confessed to me, would he ever come up to Stilfs with another person. I reflect that Franz, too, is standing at his window and observing him, that Olga is observing him from up on the first floor, that Roth is probably also observing him from a window in the stables. Whenever the Englishman is here, he infects us with his restlessness. We are indebted to him for stimulation, for so much food for thought, so much news. But he does not perceive our paltriness and pitifulness. To the contrary. All his previous visits have given us much to think about, months of mental nutriment. In point of fact, he always comes at just the right moment. What could we possibly know of events down below, when we are absolutely isolated up here? In truth, it has been more than a year since Franz and I last went down to the Alz. Roth alone still maintains personal contact with the world. But he is always full of trashy rumours when he comes up from the tavern. It is Roth who takes the milk to the Alz. Roth carries the provisions that we need, matches, sugar, spices. It is Roth who reads the newspaper down in the valley. We ourselves have not read a single newspaper in years, because one day in the blink of an eye, after decades of being smitten with newspaper reading, we came to abhor the reading of newspapers and ceased to permit ourselves to read them. We strictly forbade him to bring any newspapers up here to us. But when the Englishman brings us newspapers, we pounce on them as though dying of hunger for newspaper reading. We don't listen to the radio. We enjoy listening to music, but we are never in our sister's company; at most we see her once a day, when we say *Good morning* or *Good night*. If only the Englishman knew how far we have already estranged ourselves from everything. But it would actually be pointless to tell him the truth, to tell him the truth in such a way that he would be convinced of it. For what purpose would it serve to swear to him that our existence is no longer anything but a bestial existence? It has been years since the colossal library—in which three enormous bequests of books (one from one of our great-grandfathers' brother, the doctor in Padua, one from our maternal grandfather's brother, the judge in Augsburg, and one from our uncle, our mother's brother, the mill-owner in Schärding) have been consolidated into a single enormous collection—it has been years since this colossal library was last set foot in by any of us.

If only the Englishman knew how much we loathe the very act of reading. When he is here, we mimic his interest in written matter; when he is gone, we do not take the slightest interest in it. If only he knew that we have locked up the library and thrown its key into the Alz! If only he knew that! If only he knew that we have a made a virtue of the necessity that Stilfs is to us, that the moment we realized that Stilfs marked the end of our development, we did everything in our power to accelerate this end. We are not killing ourselves, but we are accelerating our natural end, which is not a natural end at all. At Stilfs, I think, the Englishman is surrounded by benightedness. But Franz is right when he says we must not take the Englishman into our confidence, for the moment we did that we would destroy the thing in him that we find so immeasurably valuable; perhaps we would even destroy Midland himself and the consequences of that would be the very dreadful ones we dread. If the Englishman stopped coming to Stilfs, we would await his arrival in vain. We make him believe everything except the truth, but in this case nothing is more exigent than the lie. We must not make his Stilfs turn into its antithesis, into our Stilfs, in his eyes. Franz often warns me against saying too much, for nobody is more strongly tempted to say everything about Stilfs all at once than I am, because the Englishman is the person to whom I am most strongly inclined to say everything about Stilfs; the Englishman is the person, the first person, to whom I would divulge what I must not divulge to him, the truth, but it is Franz, not me, who suddenly and unwarily says or does not say what must or must not be said to Midland. Because to the extent that we do not tell the truth about our situation, and refrain from allowing anybody, even the Englishman, a glimpse into our lives, we are concealing a secret, a secret of which the Englishman is incessantly speaking even if it is diametrically opposed to what he supposes it to be. The proof of this will come and can only come from our deaths, when it will be seen that we never existed independently of disorder, of an unimaginable chaos. Call everything into question, he said yesterday. Everything is nonsense. There he goes, I think and I think, how crazy this person is, this person with whom Franz and I have nothing in common but our age and otherwise nothing but diametrically opposed qualities, this donor of unease, this caller into question. He may indeed even think, when he is thinking, what I think, namely, that everything that we—Franz and I, and he himself as well, along with everyone else in existence—are made of is over and done with, is dead. And yet basically it is this thought alone—namely, that everything that is, meaning everything that has been, is dead, that even the present, because it is, is by its very nature dead—that preoccupies all of us, all human beings, exclusively, whatever they do and wherever and whatever they are and may be and in the midst of what they call life, being, existence, getting by, getting away, or getting things done, because they are incapable describing it as anything else. Scarcely any human being is more of a stranger to us and scarcely any human being is closer to us than he is. Because he thinks in and speaks several languages and commands these languages as a highly musical and mathematical art, he is superior to us. He believes that if he had been confined to a single locale and a single field of knowledge, he would have long since managed to produce what he believes we have produced—a rational edifice of colossal dimensions. But confinement to a single field of knowledge, specialization, is not possible for him, probably because he finds it profoundly loathsome. He is a person who has to be constantly correlating everything with everything and incessantly considering everything in terms of everything. Therein lies the root of his inability to actualize any of the thousands of ideas that are constantly and quite naturally merging into one another in his brain, that brain *trained to universalize*. There he goes, I think, this man who speaks of the ancient as well as the modern humanities as if they were a compost heap, who speaks of the evil causes of painful effects. There he goes, this man in whose eyes the axis of the universe is not straight. How often this man has offended me, and how often must I have offended him, I think. For oftentimes our only means of escaping from each other is ruthlessness, is unabashed preemptive head-butting. Intellectual intimacies, the Englishman opined tonight, obtained between people like us. And to be sure, he added in so many words, unnatural ones obtained between him and me, and the most natural ones possible obtained between him and Franz. He explained himself; we understood. He said that Franz's way of thinking, his views, were diametrically opposed to his own way of thinking and views, but in a completely natural way, that my way of thinking and views were just as diametrically opposed to his way of thinking and views, but in an unnatural way. That every word that we, Franz and I, said at every moment we were together with Midland confirmed that we had different fathers. That our contrasting shared maternal kinship was decisive. That wherever, whenever we were, we bore the mark of the catastrophe, of the fact that was the most terrible fact imaginable, the fact of having been born into this world.

That in our comportment he uninterruptedly perceived the repugnance that is in truth the very stuff that we are made of. That it was this unfortunate quality that had to be bridged by every person who approached us, every person who spoke with us, even before that person came here to see us. That probably nobody had yet dared either physically or mentally to approach us in an attitude utterly devoid of suspicion. And that this suspicion, which had always been a quite specific kind of suspicion, was getting stronger with the passage of years, that someday, and indeed probably very soon, this suspicion would deteriorate into the impossibility of making any sort of contact with us whatsoever. In the complete absence of contact, but possibly in the most ideal of states, in an ideal condition reproducible by ourselves alone, we would someday, he says, be able to actualize our goal completely undisturbed. It would be wrong to describe yesterday evening's chat, which in reality was a farrago of thousands of precipitate thoughts, as a conversation. Yesterday evening we saw quite plainly that what we think is vaguely similar to what he thinks, which was precisely what we found so refreshing. But whereas last night it became quite plain that the Englishman still has a future, it also became clear to us, Franz and me, that we no longer have a future. If only one of us still had the strength to descend from Stilfs just once, to turn his back on Stilfs, to surrender ourselves to the mercy of the world below, I think, to leave Stilfs and never return again, even at the cost of incurring the accusation of having thereby committed a crime against our sister Olga, who is utterly dependent on us, of having annihilated her! What is impossible for me and too late for me ought still to be possible for Franz and not too late for him, but everything is too late for both of us. The moment when what is no longer possible, escaping from Stilfs, would have still been possible, now lies so far back in time for us that it cannot even be discerned any more. Of course, like the Englishman, we initially believed that Stilfs was our salvation, that its conditions were the ideal conditions for us, and when we saw and understood that Stilfs was not our salvation, that its conditions were not and never could be the ideal conditions for us, that to the contrary, it spelled our annihilation, we began hoping that Olga, who by then was already completely paralysed, would die. But she has not died; who knows when she will die? And now that all three of us are feebleness incarnate, there would no longer even be any point in abandoning her. It is all a question of time and this question no longer terrifies us, because we know we have reached the end and that life no longer has any meaning for us.

THE WEATHERPROOF CAPE

From the Innsbruck lawyer Enderer, our guardian, we received the following (verbatim) account . . . for twenty years, mainly in the Saggengasse and mainly at about noon, I have been crossing paths with this person without knowing who this person is; complementarily, for twenty years, mainly in the Saggengasse and mainly at about noon, this person has been crossing paths with me, without knowing who I am . . . moreover, this person hails from the Saggengasse!, albeit from the *upper* Saggengasse, whereas I hail from the *lower* Saggengasse; both of us grew up in the Saggengasse and in fact, I think, I have always seen this person without knowing that he hails from the Saggengasse and without knowing who he is; complementarily this person has known nothing about me . . . now it occurs to me that there is something about this person that I should have noticed years ago, that I should have noticed his weatherproof cape . . . reproachfully I say to myself, we cross paths with a person for years, decades, without knowing who this person is and if we ought to notice anything about the person, we notice nothing about the person, and we could cross paths with such a person over the course of an entire life without noticing anything about the person . . . suddenly we notice something about this person with

whom we have been crossing paths for two decades, we notice
something, be it his weatherproof cape, be it something else
entirely; suddenly I noticed this person's weatherproof cape and
in connection with this I suddenly realized that this person lived
in the Saggengasse and was partial to taking walks along the
Sill . . . a week ago this person accosted me in the Herrengasse
and the man went up with me into my office; as we were climbing
the stairs I realized, you have been seeing this person for two full
decades, always the same person, always the same ageing individual in the Saggengasse, at about noon in this weatherproof
cape, in this quite ordinary but quite definitely worn-out
weatherproof cape; still, as we were climbing the stairs it was not
yet apparent to me why the person's weatherproof cape in particular was arousing my attention; suddenly, at close quarters,
the man's weatherproof cape was arousing my undivided attention . . . but it really is quite an ordinary weatherproof cape, I
thought; there are tens of thousands of such weatherproof capes
in these mountains; tens of thousands of weatherproof capes
worn by the Tyrolians . . . no matter who these people are, no
matter what they do, when they come here they all sport these
weatherproof capes; some of them sport the grey ones, and the
rest of them the green ones, because they all wear these weatherproof capes, and the numerous loden factories in the valleys just
keep thriving; these weatherproof capes are exported to every
corner of the world, but there was something quite distinctive
about the weatherproof cape of my new client: its buttonholes
were trimmed in goat leather! I have seen these goat leather-
trimmed buttonholes only once before in my life, namely, on the
weatherproof cape of my uncle, who drowned eight years ago in

the lower Sill . . . to think that this person is wearing exactly the same weatherproof cape as my drowned uncle's, I think as I am walking up to my office with the man . . . suddenly I recall that when they pulled my Uncle Worringer out of the Sill, opinion had been divided over whether his drowning had been an act of desperation or an accident, but I am firmly of the belief that it was with so-called *suicidal intent* that Worringer threw himself into the Sill; for me there can be no doubt about it; Worringer killed himself; everything in his life and ultimately everything in his *business* life points to suicide . . . by the time they were looking for the drowned man upstream of the glass factory, he had already been washed up onto the riverbank downstream of Pradl; the newspapers devoted entire pages to the incident; our entire family was hauled into public view by the press; the phrases a ruined *business*, ruined *timber*, the death of a *sawmill*, and finally *financial* and *social* ruin haunted the journalists' sensation-mongering minds . . . the funeral in Wilten was one of the biggest there has ever been; I remember thousands of people in attendance, writes Enderer . . . it's remarkable, I say to the man with whom I was climbing the staircase leading to my office, that I can't get your weatherproof cape out of my mind; several times I've failed to get your weatherproof cape out of my mind . . . your weatherproof cape, believe it or not . . . I could not help thinking but did not say, there is the most intimate connection between your weatherproof cape and my uncle; who knows whether the man knows what I am talking about, I thought and I invite the man to step into the office; step inside! I say, because the man is hesitating; next I am in the office and taking off my coat and the man is coming in . . . it very much looks as though the man was waiting for me in the front doorway of the building; today I am running twenty minutes late, I think, and then: what does this man want? I was alternately irritated by his taciturnity and his weatherproof cape; as soon as we were both inside the office, I saw even more clearly, more distinctly, after I had turned the light on, that the buttonholes of the man's weatherproof cape were trimmed with goat leather, with black goat leather, and I discerned that my new client's weatherproof cape had been tailored exactly like the weatherproof cape of my Uncle Worringer, *tailored in the simplest style*. I tell the man he must take a seat, that first thing of all I must see to the heating of the office, that I am alone, that my secretary is ill, influenza, I say, the flu; I must light a fire, but last night I got everything ready in advance, I say, so that getting the office heated won't present the slightest difficulties now; I tell the man he must take a seat; he takes a seat; this dreary fog-saturated atmosphere, I say, everything is obscured in gloom, this time of the year exacts the utmost discipline, one *must master oneself and get through it*; the sentence was rapidly uttered, for all its weightiness; at the same time I thought, what a preposterous sentence, these superfluous, preposterous matutinal sentences, I thought; everything is subjected to a colossal test of its endurance, I say, the body, the intellect, the mind, the intellect, the body. Quite naturally when people come in here, they keep their coats on, and my new client is likewise keeping on his weatherproof cape; now in the office he seemed to feel even colder than in the doorway; it won't be long before it warms up, I say; once the heat is on, I say, the warmth spreads quickly; I made a point of emphasizing to him the excellent quality of American cast-iron stoves; I made a remark about the insalubriousness of central heating; I kept saying, it's much too dark for office work; one can part the curtains, but it doesn't do any good, turn on more lamps, but it doesn't do any good; there is, I thought, a certain uncanniness about this situation, about being in my gloomy office in the morning with a strange person, a person who is completely wrapped up in his weatherproof cape, but when one considers, I say, that the shortest day of the year is only four weeks from now; I said this to no effect; I spoke about every possible thing while I was standing at the stove, but I was exclusively preoccupied with my new client's weatherproof cape. Wilten never saw anything like it, I say, thousands of people; the new client gives me the impression that he is a real-estate agent, a purchaser of properties, these people sport such weatherproof capes in such a posture and have these kinds of faces, I thought; or the man is a livestock dealer, I think; I immediately thought, he is a real-estate agent, one of these men who roam around in their weatherproof capes and look like the poorest of the poor and yet dominate the entire real-estate market of the inner Alps; on the other hand, the man may be a livestock dealer, because of course he has also kept his hat on, I think, which suggests that he is a livestock dealer; I didn't get a look at his hands; his head was very thin; you can recognize the livestock dealers from the fact that they keep their hats on even when they step into a lawyer's office; they sit down immediately and keep their hats on; the man had introduced himself to me on the staircase, I thought, but I had forgotten his name, but now I thought: a common name, a typically Tyrolian name. Suddenly I remembered that the man's name was Humer. Humer? I ask; Humer, says the man. I wanted to know what he wanted, but I did not say: *what brings you to me?*, and I did not think *what brings you to me* either; I simply said: this law firm is the oldest law firm in all of Innsbruck. My father ran this law firm before me, he ran it more as a notary's office, I said, on the one hand it is an advantage when a law firm is already quite old, on the other hand it is a disadvantage; I asked myself, why are you saying this?; the preposterousness of this utterance struck me even as I was uttering it, but that didn't prevent me from immediately uttering yet another piece of preposterousness; I said: the location of this office is ideal. But as for the effect of this utterance, or even the preceding one, on the new client—and that undoubtedly is what he is, I thought—there was no visible trace of any such effect. Because the man remained obdurately silent, and, on the other hand, I was too pressed for time to let him continue being silent—entire mountains of documents for me to attend to had piled up over the course of the past few weeks—I said: people come to me when *they have some local matter to address*. In such cases one must be intimately familiar with the ins and outs of the city, I said, and I attempted to tidy up the clutter on top of my desk; *documents, nothing but documents*, I said; thoughtlessness and indifference cause one to speak an unending succession of sentences, sentences and vestiges of sentences, such lifeless sentences and such lifeless vestiges of sentences, but I had said *documents, nothing but documents* to Humer for the first time, and simultaneously I was thinking: the man has noticed that you have already said *documents, nothing but documents* hundreds and thousands of times. I suddenly got quite exasperated by the whole situation and glancing at my watch, I said: we must get down to business. But it was quite a long time indeed before we got down

to business. This was because instead of divulging to me the reason for his presence in my office, the man now made several
remarks that struck me as being completely insignificant and also
unconnected to each other—remarks about his parentage, the
suburb he had been born in, his isolated, utterly haphazard
upbringing, his deplorable childhood, and so forth; he said something about his business relationships, said that he could not
afford to buy a train ticket to visit his sister in Linz; he talked
about some hospital stays, about some difficult operations on his
internal organs, in describing which operations he kept uttering
the words *kidney* (in connection with colds) and *liver* (owing to
alcoholism); he said that all his life he had enjoyed walking up
and down along the Sill, *not up and down along the Inn*, he
expressly emphasized, *but up and down along the Sill*; he said that
ultimately life was nothing but a repetition of repetition, that it
very rapidly exhausted itself in monotony. I suddenly got the
impression that I was dealing with a madman, with one of those
thousands of madmen who roam the Tyrolian valleys and gorges
with their madness and never manage to find an exit from their
madness (from Tyrol). I now said that it really would be all right
by me if he, Humer, were to tell me the reason for his presence
in my office. Whereupon Humer said: I am the owner of the
funerary draper's shop in the Saggengasse. He said that he had
already come to the door of my office twice, but as everybody
knew that lawyers had a lot of things to do in court, and that it
was scarcely possible to catch up with them in their offices, he
had waited for me downstairs in front of the front door of the
building . . . Even as the office was rapidly warming up, I got
the feeling that the man was getting colder and colder; he was

withdrawing further and further into his weatherproof cape . . . the old, thick walls, I said; I was about to say the old thick walls never get warm, but I did not say that, because it struck me as preposterous to say that, so I simply said: the old, thick walls. I think, my uncle's weatherproof cape had six buttonholes; I immediately count the buttonholes on Humer's weatherproof cape and count them yet again, a third time, always from top to bottom and from bottom to top and I think, Humer's weatherproof cape also has got six buttonholes, six buttonholes trimmed with black goat leather, which leads me to think that this cape *must* be my Uncle Worringer's . . . but I did not say that, because it struck me as preposterous to say that, but I do immediately say something about the weatherproof cape while saying something about the upper Saggengasse; *when it comes to coping with these constant inundations of the upper Saggengasse by river-floods*, I said, Humer nodded, I said, no garment is more useful than a weatherproof cape like yours; granted, everybody wears these weatherproof capes, I said, but your weatherproof cape is a special weatherproof cape; it has buttonholes trimmed with goat leather. But Huber did not react to this at all; or, rather, he did not react to it as I had expected him to. He said he had never sought out a lawyer before, that I was the first, the *first available one*, he confessed; there had been no recommendation, he said, no, no recommendation. For twenty years I kept crossing paths with you, he said, but I never realized you were the lawyer here . . . you'll simply go to that law office, I thought, to that old law office . . . Owner of the funerary draper's shop in the Saggengasse; the man is neither a real-estate agent nor a cattle dealer . . . Obviously I am familiar with your establishment, I said; what did I have to gain from telling the lie that I was *obviously* familiar with his funerary draper's shop; you are always saying things that are not true, I thought; then I thought, it makes no difference to me what the man thinks . . . for a certain amount of time a person resists seeking out legal counsel, but eventually the moment comes when he does seek out legal counsel; suddenly, a person cannot go on any longer and he goes to see a lawyer . . . the most depressed of all depressives are people who seek out a lawyer because they have no way out and doubtless Humer is such a person, I thought . . . a person's got the choice of either killing himself or going to a lawyer, says Humer, writes Enderer; when Humer said that I started to take an interest in his situation . . . now, writes Enderer, I started to take an interest in everything having to do with this case that had all of a sudden become quite distressing and invigorating . . . the man was now speaking very calmly, without the slightest degree of agitation, and I was taking notes; there were no digressions, he stuck strictly to the facts, writes Enderer, he spoke with all the unadorned monotony of a man in total despair . . . I am generally unmoved by the people who seek out my counsel, writes Enderer, but this man was an exception . . . suddenly, Humer says, writes Enderer: I recognize the people I cross paths with by their clothes; I see their clothes, not their faces. Their feet, *yes*, their faces, *no*. To begin with I look at their shoes. That's where we're different, I said, I see their faces immediately. I don't see their faces, he said. So for twenty years he didn't see my face and saw only my clothes; whereas for twenty years I saw his face but didn't see his clothes; whence, writes Enderer, the fact that I never saw his weatherproof cape . . . How long have you had that weatherproof cape of yours anyway? I said all of a sudden and Humer replied *Many years*; he did not say *four* or *five* or *three* or *eight* or *ten* or *twelve* years, as I had hoped he would; he said *Many years*; his was doubtless a completely worn-out but for all that *still-warm* weatherproof cape, I thought, exactly eight years ago my uncle threw himself into the Sill; in my opinion, Humer's weatherproof cape is even older, about ten years old; my uncle's weatherproof cape was new, a year old at most . . . but I did not ask Humer where he had got the weatherproof cape from, even though it would have been the most obvious thing in the world to ask: *so where did you get that weatherproof cape from? So where did you buy that weatherproof cape?*; I did not ask; for a longish interval I continued hearing him say: *Many years*. This phrase kept nagging at me; the man could say whatever he liked, I kept hearing nothing but that phrase *Many years*, and the buttonholes are trimmed with black goat leather, I thought . . . To begin with, he looked at people's shoes, then, naturally, at the hems of their trouser legs, said Humer, writes Enderer, and because of this I never see anybody's face, because of this I never saw your (my) face, writes Enderer; this is also owing to his stooped posture, I thought; Humer's upper body was crooked; the man's spinal column was quite acutely crooked, I saw, as I observed Humer, who was no longer huddled in the weatherproof cape; it was crooked to a degree I had never before seen in anybody's spinal column . . . he said he took a keen interest in the quality of a person's shoes and the quality of his trousers, in the kind of suit and coat the person was wearing; he had an equally pronounced sensitivity to the quality of types of fabric, and also of leather . . . is it *genuine* leather, he would ask himself, calf leather, cow leather?

goat leather? or: is it perchance *an English type of fabric?* I never see the face, he said and he raised his shoulders and in so doing made himself even more miserable-looking . . . several times he repeated *never the face, never the face* . . . but *I* have quite a precise knowledge of *your* face, I said, writes Enderer; in the blink of an eye I had perceived that it was necessary for me to say something in my turn, for *me* to say *something of my own,* that Humer, who had all of a sudden said *a great deal,* was now silent and I said: I have had extremely precise knowledge of you for quite a long time now, and to this I gratuitously added *your face is utterly extraordinary;* I was immediately conscious of the awkwardness of this expression; I couldn't help thinking that my interlocutor was acutely aware of the outrageousness of expressions like *your face is utterly extraordinary* and I said: I am different from you, who always look at people's shoes and at the hems of their trouser legs; I always look straight at their faces, *into* their faces. After a pause: I take no interest in people's clothing; I am interested only in their faces and several times I repeated this, I take no interest in what people are wearing, I am interested only in their faces . . . when I am looking into their faces, I know a great deal about these people, I said, writes Enderer; I thought, these people who are running all over the place in their grey and green weatherproof capes and getting on one another's nerves in their weatherproof capes and I suddenly said aloud to my interlocutor: *when you've got a weatherproof cape like that one, there's not a storm in the world that can do you any harm!* as I said to myself, you hate everything having to do with these weatherproof capes; despite this I once again said: there is nothing more useful than a weatherproof cape like that one, and the longer you sport a weatherproof cape like that one, I said, I actually said *sport*, which is unacceptable, it is absolutely unacceptable to say *sport*, and the longer you *sport* a weatherproof cape like that one, the better; one gets used to sporting such a garment, I said; the thought that in Humer's weatherproof cape I might *actually be dealing with* the weatherproof cape of my uncle who had drowned in the Sill eight years earlier kept nagging at me; on the one hand I was interested in Humer's *fate*, on the other hand I was interested in his weatherproof cape; it was unclear to me which of the two I was more interested in, in Humer's weatherproof cape or in Humer's *fate*, but truth to tell, I was still very much more interested in Humer's weatherproof cape than in his *fate*, than in Humer's catastrophe, which had long since come to light, and hence I was still much less interested in the catastrophe of this person than in his weatherproof cape; but I did not ask: *where did you get that weatherproof cape from anyway?* it is possible, I thought, that one must ask a man like Humer *directly*; *indirectness will get you nowhere,* but I did not ask him; the whole time I deliberated whether to ask him, but I did not ask him, on the one hand I was curious what Humer's reply would be if I were to ask him: *where did you get* (buy, find, etc.) *that weatherproof cape anyway?*; on the other hand I was *fearful* of his answer; in point of fact, I was quite worried about what sort of answer it would turn out to be. I thought, writes Enderer, now don't you say anything more about the weatherproof cape, forget all about the weatherproof cape, I thought, that is quite enough about the weatherproof cape; but no sooner had I resolved to speak no further about Humer's weatherproof cape, to forget all about his weatherproof cape, to *switch off* the weatherproof cape, than I once again became pre-occupied with nothing but the weatherproof cape. And yet I did not dare to ask where Humer had got the weatherproof cape from. I did the arithmetic and said to myself: eight years ago, naturally, eight years ago, my Uncle Worringer threw himself with his weatherproof cape into the Sill and washed up onto the riverbank downstream of Pradl *without* the weatherproof cape, *without* the weatherproof cape, I thought; and as I was thinking this, instead of saying anything *to the point* or asking, where did you get that weatherproof cape from anyway?—especially given that the fact that Humer's weatherproof cape, just like my Uncle Worringer's, has six goat leather-trimmed buttonholes, unquestionably indicated that in Humer's weatherproof cape I had to be dealing with my uncle's weatherproof cape—I said, I judge people by their faces, I have no other means of forming judgements, when forming judgements about people I have nothing to go on but their faces, whereas *you* judge people by their clothes . . . in point of fact, of course even my own clothing is of substandard quality, I said, which is astonishing in a lawyer . . . the fact that his, Humer's clothing was of substandard quality was bound up with his existence, an existence that had been being eclipsed little by little and extremely painfully over the past few decades in particular; in point of fact, as he himself said, his eclipse had not started at the time of his son's wedding, but much earlier, ten or even more years earlier, he said, with the sudden tariff reduction and the radical decline in the price of crêpe paper and tissue paper, raw materials for the production of funerary drapery. In court, one obviously has to appear in first-rate clothes, I said, writes Enderer; I was conscious of the preposterousness of this expression as well, even before I uttered it, but even in court I do not wear first-rate clothes, nice clothes; that's right, I said, in court I don't wear first-rate clothes, which

THOMAS BERNHARD

makes me different, I said, writes Enderer. I had, I said, never attached any importance to first-rate clothes, or to clothes in general. What are clothes?, I said and I found the sentence virtually insufferable, but I had already uttered the sentence. I never ask myself, am I dapperly attired? I said, are my clothes of substandard quality? I never pose these questions to myself . . . the fact that I am not attired in first-rate clothes doesn't mean that I am dressed in an off-putting style and manner, I said and added: most of the time I am well dressed; what is more, I abhor tailors; I hope I am not offending you, I said, writes Enderer, when I say that I abhor tailors, *men's tailors in particular*, I said and I did not know why I said *men's tailors in particular* and I said: *I shop at the big department stores*. It all depends on your figure, I said . . . it is an open question whether I would have accomplished more if I had attached more importance to clothes, meaning any importance at all to them . . . The question, is the luck of the well-attired man better than that of the poorly attired man? is an open question . . . but questions of this kind are of no interest to me, I said, writes Enderer, then suddenly: one can buy weatherproof capes anywhere, provided one still knows where one can get discounts . . . it's one's profession, Humer then said, writes Enderer, that determines whether one can allow oneself to be negligent about one's clothing or not; it hinges on the occupation that one *practices* . . . often fine clothes are quite simply a prerequisite, I said . . . now I suddenly asked Humer to state his business once again; I said that what he had said was clear to me; that out of all his hints, his inchoate long sentences or quite simply short ones, I had been able to form an idea of his case, in other words, an idea of what it was about, of the reason why he

88

was here in my office, but that my habitual method was to have the client state his business a second time immediately after the first time; in the course of the repetition of the facts of the case, the central issue of the case comes to light, I said; everything appears in a new light, in an *incorruptible* light, I said; when one covers the first presentation of the facts of the case with the second presentation of the facts of the case, in other words, makes the attempt to cover the first and second presentation or *delineation* of the facts of the case, it often turns out that what was previously insignificant is fundamentally significant, that what was initially significant is all of a sudden insignificant and that on balance everything is really about something else entirely . . . so I now added to my earlier notes what Humer was saying *now* and I thought, I shall have the man state his business to me *several times*, not only twice, as usual, perhaps three times, perhaps four times . . . that way I will be certain of how everything fits together . . . it was necessary for him to state everything from the beginning once again, I said to Humer, writes Enderer, because although his case was already fairly clear to me, it was not yet completely clear to me by any means . . . at this point, writes Enderer, Humer did not merely utter ready-made phrases; rather, he expatiated on the particulars of his business in a logical manner and was in a position to distinguish what was important from what was unimportant, what was relevant to the facts of the case from what was irrelevant to the facts of the case, what lent credibility to the facts of the case from what only undermined them; as far as I am concerned, my practical knowledge *regarding these people and on behalf of these people* is so extensive that I am intimately familiar with their thinking and with their way of

speaking . . . on the one hand his affair was extremely complicated, on the other hand it wasn't, said Humer, writes Enderer;
with the utmost vehemence Humer described the goings-on at
his house in the Upper Saggengasse as I, because I was obliged
to add more wood to the fire, observed from the stove how he
was now even enfolding his knees more and more tightly in the
weatherproof cape; the fact that I was observing him from the
stove in the most impermissible manner, with that keenness of
attention that no human being can get away with directing at
another human being, escaped his notice, because he was staring
at the floor; with these people one never knows if they are looking at the floor because they are insecure when meeting new
people, hence, as far as Humer was concerned, because he felt
absolutely insecure in my office; for some reason or other, these
people stare at the floor, out of fear or ill breeding, out of inse-
curity or with criminal intent; I was struck by the incredibly large
size of the weatherproof cape as I observed Humer from the
stove, then additionally by his rough-hewn shoes, those
unusually rough-hewn Russia leather shoes; it occurred to me
that his trousers were of the old-fashioned sort, broad cuffs
etcetera, it occurred to me that they were frayed; strux trousers,
I thought . . . the ceremoniousness of these people is always the
same, I thought, while I was observing Humer, as he behaved as
anybody who is freezing behaves, as he pressed the buttoned-up
weatherproof cape tightly against his chest with both hands in
the characteristic cold-cramped manner of somebody helplessly
freezing in unfamiliar surroundings . . . by now I knew what we
were dealing with and I said, I know what we are dealing with,
but if you will give me a precise description, a precise enumer-
ation, of everything one more time; don't leave anything out,

don't leave anything out, I said; I shall be able to understand the case better and in order to tackle the case in the most effective way I shall need yet another delineation of all the circumstances, *all* the circumstances, I repeated . . . as mentioned earlier, on the staircase, and then in the office, I had offhandedly taken Humer for a cattle dealer or for a real-estate agent; now the thought of this error annoyed me again; the fact that you are the proprietor of a funerary draper's shop, I suddenly said—I most certainly did not intend to say this but I suddenly said it—*is something that I am obviously aware of*; again I found myself uttering this lie; Humer opined that in these houses in the Saggengasse and particularly in the upper Saggengasse, in these numerous older houses, a person went to seed; that if a person did not constantly exercise the utmost vigilance he would go under; suddenly he had sat up straight and histrionically said: *he'll go under* . . . initially in their ceremoniousness they are unready to speak, but then they let themselves go and say much more than one wishes to hear, writes Enderer, but Humer confined himself to saying things that were useful and even the remarks that I had at first taken for totally superfluous remarks on his part, remarks about his childhood, about the technique for cutting spun rayon, etcetera, were now proving to be important . . . even the fact that he had said at the very beginning that his daughter-in-law was a native of Matrei was proving to be important . . . the fact is that these people, once they have warmed up, let themselves go and are quite trust-inspiring and ultimately quite trusting in their possession of their simple but reliable approach to things, writes Enderer, that they are initially hesitant, then quite resolute, fearless, and at the stove it now struck me how useful it is to give a person like Humer a good amount of time to warm up, and not to rebuff him at the outset, not to muzzle him at the outset, not to irritate him with invasive questions as I had kept doing in such an unfortunate fashion earlier; by doing this I have always ruined everything . . . Humer was extremely unprepossessing, writes Enderer, extremely old, for I was doubtlessly dealing with a sixty-five-year-old, a nearly seventy-year-old, human being; on account of his utter wretchedness I got the impression that he was a creature, I suddenly felt certain that he was a creature; a creature is in my office . . . and I must handle this creature with the utmost circumspection . . . but then I became irritated at the thought that I had so far done no such thing, and I preoccupied myself once again with Humer's weatherproof cape . . . if the man is wearing strux trousers, I thought, he is also wearing a strux jacket, a strux coat, I thought; on account of their warmth on the one hand, on account of their cheapness on the other, such coats are very popular with the common people; in point of fact I believed I could infer from the smell of Humer's clothing that his was a completely strux outfit, strux trousers, a strux coat, a strux jacket, for undoubtedly Humer's trousers were strux trousers, as I was able to ascertain even in the semi-darkness of the office; my electric lighting is terribly dim on November mornings; the causes of this dimness are on the one hand the mountain springs, which are virtually running dry, and on the other hand the most incredibly advanced industries; strux trousers and a strux jacket, that suits his physical being down to the ground, I thought . . . and on top of all that the weatherproof cape . . . and his black hat on his head and his grey Schladminger wool socks . . . on the one hand my predicament is extremely complicated, on the other hand it isn't, he said again, writes

Enderer, and as if by way of reinforcing what he had said so far, at specific intervals he kept coming back to the starting point that was his *tragedy* (as he termed it), writes Enderer, he said: *when my son had just turned twenty-two*, he kept repeating *when my son had just turned twenty-two* and then: *when my son got married* and *when my daughter-in-law came from Matrei to live in our house* . . . every five or six or eight sentences he kept repeating *when my son had just turned twenty-two* or *when my son got married* and *when my daughter-in-law came from Matrei to live in our house*; my impression that everything Humer said was gloom-ridden, if not utterly eclipsed by darkness, was naturally only reinforced by the dim electric light and more generally by the time of the year. All of a sudden he said: because you know nothing whatsoever about me and because we have been crossing each other's paths for two decades . . . the sentence hung in the air for a rather long time, until he said: but if you are familiar with my shop . . . whereupon I, writes Enderer, said: I have never been inside your shop, in point of fact I am familiar with the funerary draper's shop in the Saggengasse by sight, but I have never been inside the shop; I wanted to leave Humer in no doubt on this point. My father bequeathed it to me forty years ago, said Humer, writes Enderer, then: things have been getting better and better for the business, and worse and worse for me. Humer repeated this sentence several times as well, writes Enderer. As regards the business, said Humer, writes Enderer, things have been improving; as regards me, they have been deteriorating. The whole thing started because he had had his son learn the funerary drapery trade, a higher form of tailoring, writes Enderer, and in point of fact, as I now know, writes Enderer, an exceedingly subtle artisanal trade, which he had had his son learn, just as Humer's father had had him learn it, Humer's grandfather had had Humer's father learn it, and so on. By the age of seventeen, they, including his son, had finished their apprenticeship, and finished it, to be sure, in the paternal shop, the only funerary draper's shop in Tyrol. One may well ask how long it has been there; nobody knows the answer to that question, writes Enderer, but in point of fact the Humers' funerary draper's shop has been on the upper Saggengasse for some eighty years. And when one knows how huge funeral expenditures are, and in particular here in Tyrol funeral expenditures are especially huge, one cannot but assume that such a shop is a good shop. And Humer makes no secret of this; as he is speaking, in everything he says, one constantly thinks one can hear him exclaiming, what a good shop! And it was this thing in particular that he was suddenly no longer able to maintain at its pinnacle of excellence that played the principal role in the events surrounding Humer. But, said Humer, writes Enderer: we even produce for the export market. As he is saying the word *export market* his voice is unsteady. As I said, said Humer, writes Enderer, I have sought you out on account of the unbearableness in which I am forced to exist. The mere fact that I, the owner of such a prosperous shop, am running around in strux trousers and in a strux overcoat, is bound to give you pause, says Humer, writes Enderer, the fact that the proprietor of a shop is in strux trousers and in a strux coat and in such rough-hewn shoes . . . that is bound to give me pause, writes Enderer and he writes: you don't know my son, says Humer, but you have seen my son quite often, probably you have seen my son even more often than you have seen me; he is constantly running through the upper Saggengasse, this tall individual in this conspicuous outfit, says Humer and then: for years my son has been frequenting the *Grey Bear*, you know what that means! My daughter-in-law from Matrei is to blame for this, for the fact that he dines at the *Grey Bear* every day while I myself must make do with the very simplest food, and my son, says Humer, writes Enderer, spends a great deal of money! And on top of that and time and again he also dines at yet another restaurant and also quite often attends the municipal theatre. One can't help wondering, says Humer, what is going on in the mind of a person like that! But the whole problem is that my son got married in a most unfortunate manner and at the most inauspicious moment, but he won't admit this; I know full well that this marriage is an unfortunate one, but he won't admit this. My son is unfortunate; this woman has made a mess of his life, says Humer, writes Enderer. What was more, by then Humer's son hadn't been frequenting the *Grey Bear* but, rather, the *Crown Imperial* for quite some time; just imagine that, says Humer, writes Enderer, he *frequents the Crown Imperial!* Because you yourself, says Humer to me, writes Enderer, dine quite often at the *Grey Bear*, as I know for a fact, you certainly must know who my son is, as I said; he is conspicuously tall and conspicuously attired, a conspicuously tall figure, says Humer, and I ask myself, writes Enderer, how Humer happens to know that I do in point of fact dine quite often at the *Grey Bear*, as you know, Enderer writes to us; I dine at the *Grey Bear* every Saturday and Sunday; it is still the best place to dine. But naturally even at the *Grey Bear* it sometimes happens that one is served something that is not fit to be eaten, writes Enderer and he adds: Humer says that his daughter-in-law has abnormally long hair, and that she is constantly, writes Enderer, says Humer, *unkempt; my daughter-in-law is always unkempt,* there is, by the way, nothing I hate more than a person who is unkempt, says Humer, but the mere fact that she is unkempt is not the cause of my aversion, says Humer; thanks to this woman, who hails from the *lowest social class*; her father is still active as a house painter in Matrei, says Humer; her mother helps them make ends meet as a cleaning woman; *as* he is saying this, his voice is filled with the utmost extremity of contempt, writes Enderer; as I said, for some time now the two of them have been frequenting the *Crown Imperial*, writes Enderer; at the *Crown Imperial* they pay twice as much for everything as at the *Grey Bear*, Humer says and I think, with my money, says Humer, in no time at all, Humer now says, because they live more for pleasure than for business, they will have squandered everything, and to squander a shop like my shop, *it still belongs to me, of course!* Humer exclaims, *it still belongs to me*, and, he adds, so does a large portion of stupidity and the hatred of a father. I had heard him correctly, Humer told me, *the hatred of a father*, Humer says, and then: sixteen sewing machines, sir, if you can imagine it, sixteen sewing machines so far and I thought, writes Enderer, sixteen people at sixteen sewing machines; we deliver on a contractual basis, says Humer, writes Enderer, to Vorarlberg and Salzburg as well and recently also to Bavaria; in Bavaria funerary drapery is twice as expensive as it is here; there they can charge a much higher tariff on the funerary drapery received by forty undertakers from Humer's workshop in the upper Saggengasse, writes Enderer. And everything that I have built up over decades my son is squandering in the company of his raffish wife over the briefest amount of time imaginable, and he frequents the *Crown Imperial!*, says Humer, then Humer continues: as far as I am concerned, the factual findings are as follows: such a turn of phrase proves that Humer, during the brief amount of time he has been in my presence here in my office—and if it is true that I am the first lawyer in his life, writes Enderer, and I do not doubt the veracity of the information he has given me; this person is telling the truth, and is immeasurably aurally attentive; these ears of his have all along given me the impression that they hear everything, including what I do *not* say—such a turn of phrase proves that Humer is already familiar with legalese and that he is now already speaking legalese when he says, the factual findings are as follows: whereas I, as you know—and as I do in point of fact already know, because Humer has said this several times already—whereas I, Humer then says, lived for thirty years in peace and quiet on the ground floor, by which I mean in an apartment next door to my shop in the Saggengasse; from the first breath I ever took onwards, he says with great passion, I lived in this ground-floor apartment, a few more times he insistently says, from my first moments onwards, all the while gesticulating with his hands, which now all of a sudden are no longer clinging to his weatherproof cape, and speaking ever more vehemently and also stretching out his relatively long legs; slowly Humer stretched out his relatively long legs, writes Enderer, his entire long, lean body relaxed, now that the man had begun to speak of his ground-floor apartment in the Saggengasse, out of a cramped position in which it had been sitting for at least an hour; in point of fact, Humer has now been sitting in my office for over an hour, and the fact that he is even sitting here at all, I suddenly think, was made possible only by the fact that in forgetting that on this morning of the week I absolutely never keep office hours, I let him come up here into my office, in forgetting to think no office hours today! I simply invited the man to come up here with me into the office; thanks to the way and manner in which the man had been standing downstairs in the front doorway—he is doubtless waiting for me because of something important, I thought, the man has come on important business, without asking myself whether it made sense, whether it was worthwhile, to let the man come up here—I invited him to come up here, writes Enderer; of course there are never any office hours on Monday I thought, writes Enderer, and I suddenly said to Humer *of course there are never any office hours on Monday!*, but he did not react to this; he continued sitting there, now he was sitting completely upright, writes Enderer, suddenly his spine was perfectly straight and he spoke of his ground-floor apartment, a very lovely apartment, sir, he said. When one has grown up in such a spacious ground-floor apartment, and now once again he was in the realm of *actuality*, writes Enderer, one can't just move out of an apartment that is completely suited to one's needs overnight. He said he had been accustomed to being around everything in this apartment since his earliest childhood, writes Enderer; he is on the most intimately familiar terms with everything in this apartment, and a person who is accustomed to living in a ground-floor apartment cannot, all of a sudden after decades and moreover for the most threadbare reason, be thrown out of his ground-floor apartment; believe me, says Humer, writes Enderer; there is nothing more horrible. They threw me out of my ground-floor apartment. Overnight. He, Humer, had to move up into the first floor, they had told him, writes Enderer and Humer says: my daughter-in-law from Matrei is behind the whole thing, because my son, sir, never would have thrown me out; he is too weak to do that; my son could never do such a thing. But, writes Enderer: sons get married, said Humer, and are soon as ruthless and ruthless in the same way as their wives, and a marriage to a woman like my daughter-in-law spells the dissolution of a business, spells *its annihilation*. Under the pretext of expanding the shop (of acquiring a wood-pulp storage room twice as large as the existing one!), my son compelled me to move out of my ground-floor apartment and up to the first floor. But he did not set up a larger wood-pulp storage room, says Humer, then, gradually, I saw that he was most certainly not setting up a larger wood-pulp storage room and I pointed out to him that I had moved out of the ground-floor apartment only because he had been planning to set up a larger wood-pulp storage room, whereupon he spoke of a coffin division that he was planning to open at the funerary draper's shop; he said that he had already applied for the license, but that the regional government was taking its time; finally I found out that my son had most certainly not applied for a license for a coffin division. What lies he tells! said Humer, writes Enderer. First, a larger wood-pulp storage room, then, a coffin division, then: space for six more seamstresses! which, however, also was a lie, for to this day I have not seen a single one of the six new seamstresses; to the contrary, instead of employing eighteen seamstresses as we did *as recently as two years ago*, today we employ only sixteen. And now he suddenly says, says Humer, writes Enderer, that from now on we won't be able to live off our income from the funerary draper's shop alone; such a thing is being said by a person who dines at the *Crown Imperial* and doesn't dine there alone but, rather, as half of a couple, and spends thousands there! From the moment at which he had been obliged to take his daughter-in-law into his house onwards, everything about his son had consisted of lies and *nothing but lies*. But one can't win if one is fighting against a person like my daughter-in-law, says Humer, writes Enderer; everything is just going to keep getting worse. Now in point of fact Humer could have refused to move out of his ground-floor apartment, writes Enderer, but such a refusal is pretty much beyond the strength of a man like Humer, just as it is pretty much beyond the strength of any man. After all, the shop still ultimately belongs to me! says Humer. But once his son is married, a father can no longer do as he wishes in his own house. He still did not know the *full extent of the catastrophe*, these were Humer's exact words, the catastrophe that could actually ensue only now that I have moved out of my ground-floor apartment and up into the first floor. In exhaustion Humer says, writes Enderer: and I moved up to the first floor. For days I told myself I wouldn't move up there, and then I moved up there anyway. And once I was living upstairs, I saw that it was all a bunch of lies, nothing but lies, that I had been taken in by a bald-faced lie. They didn't just suggest to me that I should move out; they threw me out, genuinely threw me out, repeated Humer several times. With difficulty, but little by little, he had managed to get used to the first floor, he said, writes Enderer and Humer began to unbutton his weatherproof cape. As he was unbuttoning the weatherproof cape—it was now no longer warm; it was hot—I noticed a fairly large tailor's insignia on the lining of the weatherproof cape, the same tailor's insignia I remember from my uncle's weatherproof cape. Or was I mistaken? writes Enderer, is it perhaps not the same tailor's insignia after all?, I thought, and by then the tailor's insignia was no longer in view, for Humer had suddenly folded the weatherproof cape in such a way, folded it down from his left shoulder and from his right shoulder in such a way that the tailor's insignia was no longer in view. In point of fact he, Humer, Enderer writes further, discovered certain so-called perks to living on the first floor. As you know, says Humer, in all these houses and above all in the houses in the Saggengasse, it is humid on the ground floor but on the first floor it is dry. He had immediately been able to observe an alleviation of his rheumatism (he said, an improvement of my rheumaticism, he did not say rheumatism but, rather, rheumaticism), in other words, he could perceive an alleviation of his rheumatic symptoms, writes Enderer. He had arrived at the conviction that he was finding it advantageous to have moved out of the ground-floor apartment and up to the first floor. Within the first few days there was likewise an improvement of my back pain, says Humer. But I said nothing about this, to keep them (my children) from exploiting it, for if I had admitted that I was enjoying even the slightest advantage, they would have immediately exploited that. All of a sudden I became capable of walking faster, of bending over and even of bending over all the way to the floor, and I had been incapable of doing that for decades; he was enjoying greater and *virtually pain-free* mobility altogether on the first floor. But I didn't say a word about it, said Humer, to the contrary. I also observed that the first floor gets more light. You don't need as many light-bulbs; the air is better; there is more oxygen, less noise. But the fact that he could not keep as close an eye on how business was going downstairs in the shop, and thus on the machinations going on there, as he had been able to from his ground-floor apartment, was galling to him. In the first-floor apartment I was completely cut off from the shop; they—his son and his daughter-in-law—were counting on my not being able to come down from the first floor into the shop at every given moment to inspect things; they were working all of this into their calculations, all of it, my immobility, my difficulty in getting up and down those steep stairs. It was all calculation, he said. Calculation and deception. I was cut off on the first floor; indeed, from there I could no longer even hear the ringing of the doorbell of the shop, says Humer, which increased my suspiciousness. The deception managed to spread unchecked beneath me as I sat upstairs on the first floor, and you will of course see *how* it managed to spread unchecked once you have read the papers I have brought here. Thanks to the disastrous influence of his wife my son had all of a sudden become capable *of anything*. Everything was entrenched behind lies, says Humer, writes Enderer. A colossal tactical dissimulation, says Humer. Apart from that, though, he had quickly gotten *well past his initial difficulties* and acclimatized to his new situation, to living on the first floor. But then, after three months, what he had already mentioned to me and what I had already anticipated was suggested to me, namely, that I should move out of the first floor and up to the second floor; all of a sudden I was now supposed to move out of the first floor and up to the second, says Humer, writes Enderer. Round-the-clock hatred of me, my son's hatred, my daughter's hatred. Solely and uniquely aside from my walks up and down the Saggengasse, there was nothing but hatred towards me, *who I still am there*. They said a child was on its way. Even before all this there was nothing I feared more, sir, says Humer, writes Enderer, than the moment when somebody would start talking about a child; once a child is on the scene, married couples don't split up as readily as before, but even without a child they would have been past the point of being able to split up, because my daughter-in-law is the most calculating of females. So there was talk of a child and of no longer being able to make do with their present living space once the child had arrived; now it was about the forthcoming child, at first it had been about setting up a wood-pulp storage room, then about a storage room for coffins, but whereas the wood-pulp and coffin-storage rooms had been lies, says Humer, writes Enderer, I actually believed that the child was on its way. Not a single night of sleep, says Humer, writes Enderer, a child, a child. But I didn't put up any fight to speak of and moved up to the second floor that very day, said Humer; the hard part had been getting the furniture up the very narrow stairs to the second floor, but they actually did bring all the furniture up to the second floor; I did not doubt for an instant that the child was a real child, says Humer; indeed, I could not but believe that the child already existed; all of a sudden I figured out something: *if* the child *does* indeed already exist, *then so much ado being made in such a painful way is absurd*, I said, writes Enderer, and Humer continues: my grandchild was coming, but I naturally could not figure out why I had to move up to the second floor on account of my grandchild, but I had resigned myself to the fact that I would definitely be on the second floor; that was my sacrifice to make, sir, says Humer, writes Enderer, even if it wasn't at all clear to me why. On the second floor it is even drier than on the first and the air is even better than on the first and you can hardly hear any noise at all up there. But the shop downstairs—which I was taking an ever-greater interest in, meaning a much more intense interest than before, now that I had got wise to the machinations of my son and my daughter-in-law—and everything having to do with the shop downstairs, had now slipped even further away from me upstairs; it was too onerous to go downstairs at every given moment, says Humer, writes Enderer, and also too conspicuous, to be constantly going downstairs and back upstairs and back downstairs and back upstairs, especially given that that meant being under their hate-filled gazes! and so I hardly ever went into the shop any more, and even when I did, it was only ever for a moment at a time in order to augment my pile of circumstantial evidence, my suspicion of their deception, to accumulate fakery, says Humer, writes Enderer, to make transcriptions in terrific haste and with great circumspection without being observed, which was incredibly difficult for me, because of course my son and my daughter-in-law had in their own turn long since formed the suspicion that *I* was harbouring suspicion . . . at nights I then preoccupied myself exclusively with these papers, says Humer, because on the second floor I was left in peace, completely undisturbed, says Humer, which was certainly an advantage, says Humer, writes Enderer, who suddenly exclaims: *it was all fakery! all of it was simply fakery! The entire accounting ledger had been faked! And these fakeries weren't intended, as one might suppose, to deceive the revenue office but to deceive me!* I had no other choice left than to apply to you, says Humer to me, writes Enderer. The whole thing must be settled in court, he said, the lot of it in court, for who can even dream of being considerate when dealing with a conspiracy of children against their own father! Naturally, the second floor is the most ideal place was what I *thought*, but I *said* nothing to that effect. To the contrary. He kept quiet and played a role that he had in the meantime learnt to play to the hilt, the role of the sacrificial victim. The arduousness, the inhuman troublesomeness, of climbing up to the second floor and back down from the second floor, was something he took in his stride. There are no lifts, as you know, in the Saggengasse, no lifts, says Humer. I invited my old friends up to the second floor, he says, writes Enderer; they not only reinforced his suspicion that he was being deceived, which was patently obvious in the light of the innumerable pieces of evidence on my desk, but also his intention to present the whole affair to a lawyer, in other words, to take it to court. It has of course been years since I was last able to speak about my suspicion, says Humer; I chalk this up to my attentiveness, to my love for the shop in the Saggengasse; suddenly he cried out: *nobody has managed to take my love for my shop away from me!* writes Enderer; then, writes Enderer, Humer sits down in the armchair and wraps himself up, as well as he can, in the weatherproof cape. Now you won't ever see the tailor's insignia ever again, I thought, writes Enderer; everything now seems to indicate that he won't take the weatherproof cape off again; to the contrary, from now on he is just going to keep wrapping himself up in the weatherproof cape, wrapping himself up in it more and more tightly, whereas Humer actually then extracted from the weatherproof cape a package tied together with string and placed it on my desk. They are all additional proofs, additional pieces of circumstantial evidence, he said, writes Enderer. And now, please note, says Humer, writes Enderer, and it was only now that Humer divulged to me: a week ago I was suddenly told that I should move out of the second floor as well and *into the third floor*! My son made this curious proposal to me while I was plumb in the middle of intently perusing sales brochures for wood pulp and ironing paper. Not for a moment did I doubt that although my son was asking me to move out of the second floor, says Humer, it was in reality most certainly my daughter-in-law who was asking me to do so via his insolent mouth. I said yes, says Humer and he adds that at the time he tried hard to stay calm, to avoid getting excited; well, so it was now out of the second floor and into the third! And he says he repeated the phrase several times: and into the third, and into the third, because in the interim two more children had been born; a fourth child is on its way . . . a fourth child, Humer says to me, writes Enderer, isn't that preposterous? Isn't that preposterous and mindless to boot? Several times Humer says to me: isn't that the utmost limit of mindlessness? A criminal outrage, a fourth child! says Humer, writes Enderer. In this day and age, I said, says Humer, writes Enderer, in which there are hundreds of millions of surplus human beings, a fourth child? Then, by his own account, he is supposed to have exclaimed several times: a fourth child! A fourth child! And a fifth child! And a sixth child! And a seventh child! And an eighth child! And so on! And so on! Several times: And so on! And so on! From upstairs, says Humer, writes Enderer, I heard my daughter-in-law downstairs saying: if he doesn't move up to the third floor, he will have to go into the old-people's home! From upstairs I heard her saying this downstairs, says Humer, writes Enderer. And my son says, says Humer: you are going to move to the third floor! Whereupon he, Humer, says, he lost control of himself and cried as loud as he could: a fourth child! A fourth child! To the third floor! To the third floor! A fourth child! A fifth child!, and so forth and then simply repeated: children! children! children! until he was completely exhausted, writes Enderer; then Humer says, writes Enderer: I couldn't help thinking, your son doesn't understand you, doesn't understand you any more and: just look at what this woman has turned your son into. And Humer stood up, writes Enderer, and he began pacing up and down the office and every now and then he would point at his package of papers on my desk and say: *it's all already thoroughly grounded in criminology, all already thoroughly grounded in criminology. It's all already ready for the courtroom! There's no turning back,* he says, *no turning back.* Suddenly, says Humer, writes Enderer, I said: *no, not to the third floor, not to the third floor. Categorically not! I won't move into those rooms unfit for human habitation!* I said, says Humer, writes Enderer, *I won't move up into those gloomy cubbyholes.* Then, writes Enderer, he says he left the house and walked for hours up and down along the Sill; then, Enderer writes, Humer says: and when I got back home, my son had already hauled the majority of my belongings up to the third floor, which meant up to the attic. I immediately saw this and said to myself, says Humer, writes Enderer, he has already hauled almost all your belongings to the third floor, he has hauled everything up there. And then they, my son and daughter-in-law, had also already begun to haul my furniture from the second floor up to the third floor; if you live in the Saggengasse, Humer says to me, writes Enderer, then you of course know how things look on the third floor; the third floor of each and every house in the Saggengasse looks *completely unsuitable for habitation*; he said this several times: *completely unsuitable for habitation. We'll fix them up, make them inhabitable,* they said, says Humer. And everything would have to be done *immediately*, everything *immediately*. The furniture and their father would have to go straight up to the attic, sir, says Humer, writes Enderer. They jerry-rigged two folding screens for me and tried to talk me into believing the attic was inhabitable. We have winterized the whole place up here well enough for now, says my son, says Humer, writes Enderer, and when it gets cold and starts snowing, we can heat the place up, says my son. And just imagine, says Humer, all the while my son and his wife are shifting my furniture this way and that in the attic, I can't speak, *it's as if I had lost the power of speech*, says Humer, I *want* to but I *cannot* speak; I stand there wrapped up in my weatherproof cape and cannot say a thing. And to think of *how* I suddenly had to stay silent! That horrifying, nauseating attic stench, which I have loathed from childhood onwards, says Humer. Nothing but mildew, nothing but dirt and mildew. My son is constantly saying the word *remodel*, says Humer, writes Enderer, over and over again *remodel, make them heatable*. Eventually they got all my furniture in place in the attic and also made my bed, and I was obliged to look on *without moving a muscle*; I found it impossible to chase them away; I couldn't budge a single step, couldn't say a single word, says Humer, writes Enderer. During the remodelling I am supposed to go stay with my sister in Hall, they said, says Humer, writes Enderer; in the interim you will go to Hall, I can hear my son saying, says Humer. But I thought, I'm not going to Hall, not to Hall, not to Hall, I thought. Over and over again: *not to Hall*. And suddenly: take it to court now!, go find a lawyer now and take it to court! and he says he ran out of the house and all the way to the end of the Saggengasse and into a guesthouse in the Gänsbacherstraße and from there several times to the Sill and back and to the Inn and back and finally spent the night at the guesthouse in the Gänsbacherstraße. He says that he has already been here in the Herrengasse twice and waited for me each time. *Go find that lawyer*, he thought to himself; he doesn't know why, but he kept thinking, *go find that lawyer*, again and again, *go find that lawyer*, again and again: *go find Enderer*. Day after day I kept the papers hidden close to my body, says Humer, writes Enderer, constantly hidden under my weatherproof cape; these pieces of circumstantial evidence, he says and then he says: if these papers don't suffice! whereupon I, writes Enderer, say: naturally, everything quite unquestionably follows from the papers. *File a lawsuit, file a lawsuit*, he had kept saying over and over again, he said, file a lawsuit against my son and my daughter-in-law. Suddenly he stood up and left, writes Enderer. I had called Mr Humer! after him, because I had forgotten to have him sign the form granting me full power of attorney; I had called Mr Humer!, but by then he was already gone, already downstairs. He will come back, I thought and I started trying to get through the work that I had so sorely neglected for so many weeks. But all the while I was thinking of nothing but Humer. Several crimes and misdemeanours, I thought, which on the one hand are the usual order of the day among small businessmen, and which have been committed against Humer on the other and I got more and more annoyed by the fact that I had not asked Humer about the origin of his weatherproof cape earlier. I had completely forgotten to ask him about it, although I had firmly resolved to do so. The tailor's insignia is the proof, I thought. What had Humer said? For a long time I stood on your doorstep and waited for you, says

Humer, writes Enderer, I can still hear him saying this, writes Enderer; *shall I ring the doorbell or not*, he thought; *I won't ring it*, he thought at one instant, then at the next, *I will ring it*, and over and over again, he thought, *only Enderer will do* and *is it reasonable?* or *is it not reasonable?* until I finally rang the bell . . . and then I was *obliged* to go upstairs with you to your office, once you were suddenly standing right in front of me . . . *to file a lawsuit against my son!* said Humer, writes Enderer. At first people drop hints, then they let the whole thing out, I think, writes Enderer; it is always the same, the truth is said and yet it isn't the truth . . . I should never have come up here to see you, says Humer several times, as I now remember, writes Enderer, I should never have come to see you in this condition and he says: I never should have brought this into public view! for nothing is more horrible than bringing something, no matter what it is, into public view; this is what he, Humer, says he feels, and he says that despite feeling this he won't take anything back, that he will press on and say everything, that from now on he won't hold anything back, that from now on he will stop at nothing . . . *I shouldn't have bothered you*, on the one hand, and *I have brought this into public view*, on the other . . . how could you possibly help an old man in the midst of his despair, then again: as far as I am concerned, it may very well be the most insignificant thing in the world; on the other hand, it is killing me, writes Enderer regarding Humer. Everything having to do with human beings and everything they do and try to come up with, he says, is bogus, and he adds that when one considers it thoroughly, all of life itself is bogus . . . just think of the whole thing as an episode, Humer also said, an episode having nothing whatsoever to do with you . . . for twenty years we regularly crossed each other's paths and never made each other's acquaintance and now we have made each other's acquaintance . . . *but I refuse to call off anything*, several times, several times he quite decisively said: *but I refuse to call off anything* . . . as decisively as he had said: *it is the most horrible thing in the world to bring something into public view*, he again said: *but I refuse to call off anything!* Enderer writes and draws our attention to an article in last Tuesday's *Tiroler Nachrichten* in which it is reported that on the preceding Friday, one H., a businessman, threw himself from the third floor of a house on the Saggengasse. I immediately think, that is Humer, writes Enderer and I look into the matter and in point of fact Humer did throw himself out of a window of the attic of his house on Friday before last. He died instantly, writes the reporter in the newspaper, writes Enderer. But the thing, writes Enderer, which kept nagging at him and to which he, Enderer, felt it his duty to draw our attention after reading the newspaper article, had not been Humer, had not been this life history—a life history that was, as Enderer writes, to all appearances quite extraordinary and indeed extraordinarily devastating but was in reality the quite mundane life history of an ultimately very simple man—but rather the weatherproof cape that this person had been wearing and he, Enderer, got dressed—it was, he writes, already four in the afternoon and hence already dark; everybody knows that November days are short and are actually not days at all—and went into the upper Saggengasse and into Humer's funerary draper's shop and immediately said who he, Enderer, was and that he had come on account of the deceased's weatherproof cape. Regarding the deceased's weatherproof cape, naturally I did not say the *suicide*'s weatherproof cape, writes Enderer: it happens to be the weatherproof cape of my uncle, who drowned in the Sill eight years ago, I said. By chance, I said, I came to learn that the deceased's weatherproof cape happened to be my uncle's weatherproof cape. I said nothing of Humer's visit to my office, because I personally regarded his entire case as closed. The young man in the shop, undoubtedly the deceased's son, acted as if he was familiar with the circumstances surrounding his father's weatherproof cape and hence with those surrounding my uncle's weatherproof cape and he said, yes, the weatherproof cape washed up onto the bank of the Sill a couple of years ago. Whereupon, writes Enderer, I said: as I know for a fact, your father used to walk up and down along the Sill every day. Yes, says the young man and he takes hold of the clothes rack and hands the deceased's weatherproof cape over to me without further ado . . .

UNGENACH

7 April

... at night on the fourth, on my way to Zurich, from which I am going to fly back to the USA, at my Uncle Zumbusch's in Chur, where I was planning to rest for a few days.

But as my uncle is not even in Chur—obviously because, as I realized only today, he is at my guardian's funeral—I have been more or less left to fend for myself, preoccupied time and again in all my thoughts with Ungenach, with its liquidation, its dispersal, etc...

and I am in a room from which on a clear day Mrs Morath, who cooks for me, enjoys a view of the Splügen Pass, and because it is cold (three degrees centigrade) and raining unrelentingly and I have no key to the library, or even access to newspapers, I have been preoccupied all the while with my half-brother Karl's notes, which until yesterday were in the possession of Moro the notary in Gmunden...

... which notes Moro at my request has handed over to me; and in the midst of my perusal of my half-brother's notes, which he jotted down partly in Africa, partly at Ungenach, partly on his way from Ungenach to Africa or on his way from Africa to Ungenach, I have from time to time been jotting down some notes of my own . . .

incessantly freezing, because the city of Chur is one of the coldest in existence, the gloomiest city I know, and the inhabitants of the Grisons are deep—or weak—or simply preposterous owing to the gloom and cold, and in Chur, but especially in my Uncle Zumbusch's house, when it is raining unrelentingly as it is now, people must heat their houses, even in the summer; but I have pitched up in a room that has no stove and hence cannot be heated at all; nevertheless, it is useful to be staying here.

Deafened by the waterfall beneath my window, I noted: having arrived at Ungenach (on 3 April), I immediately saw that Ungenach was completely deserted and that I had arrived too late for my guardian's funeral, which I had all the while feared missing and yet also kept trying to dissuade myself from attending . . . and I firmly resolved not to go to Ungenach nor hence to Aurach, which is a good ten kilometres away from it and where my guardian's funeral was doubtless just then taking place, but rather, at that very moment, because I certainly had no intention of seeing my relatives but merely an unrelenting revulsion from ever seeing them, and because I certainly had no desire to converse with them about anything, and least of all about Ungenach, to go see Moro the notary in Gmunden . . .

. . . to whom from Stanford I had already disclosed my intention of relinquishing, dispersing, everything having to do with Ungenach (i.e. of effectuating this entire dispersal, because

Ungenach is no longer anything but a terrifying burden to me; a dispersal that Moro the notary still finds outrageous and that everybody will probably find outrageous once word of it gets out), which, in virtue of my guardian's untimely death and the year-old discovery of my half-brother Karl's murder, has passed into my possession entirely, hence legally as well as practically, or rather practically as well as legally . . .

and to whom, as I immediately perceived after the first sentences Moro uttered in his office on Kirchengasse, this intention of mine was already a completely familiar matter and who was even already fully aware of the celerity with which I would require my scheme to be executed.

Moro leaned back in his wing chair and said, 'To be sure, although we know that everything, the effort, the despair, the adjustment to life as a form of insanity, is pointless, as your guardian always used to put it, you see; although we know this, we wish to go on *as a consequence of this pointlessness*, and therefore either to go about with a head that runs into the billions and that in running into these billions swells in size to the point of being suspect, or, because we find that going about here and there and every now and then with this head grown suspect seems to be no longer opportune, seems simply to be no longer possible, *is* no longer possible, to go headless for long periods . . .

as we have seen, entire historical epochs, in certain cases entire half centuries or indeed whole centuries, simply rush through history headless . . . we are speed fanatics, and creative in this fanaticism . . . we are labouring in a feverish frenzy of speed, you see, which does not mean that we *have* heads, which does not mean that we do *not* have them . . . we do not know whether we are headless or not . . .

so, let us get down to business,' said Moro, 'this dispersal . . . ,' and: 'naturally, my dear Robert, we surmise that everything is a swindle . . . your guardian once put it this way: We take action and make changes, without being able to take action or to make changes . . . and have no time to smash our heads up over it, regardless of whether we have a head or not . . . contradictions,' said Moro, 'incest in the brain, a delicate mechanism of elementary particles of an absurd megalomania . . . days of morbidities . . . for we do not think, nature thinks . . . on many a day we become conscious of the unbearableness; we extemporize, we paralyse . . . a sudden natural *intensity* succeeds natural *weakness*, as your guardian always used to put it: the surrealism of generations as a form of the surrealism of nature . . .

we have,' said Moro, 'a noticeably heightened power of comprehension. Our understanding is criticism. Our head is the logical product of a tautology . . . because everything is aiming at annihilation . . .

let us get down to business,' said Moro, 'a revolutionary element, this dispersal . . . wherein we descry revolutionary elements . . . Let us get down to business: it is possible that you yourself are perceiving this circumstance, the fact that you have already been sitting here for two hours while your family, or, let us say, those whom you yourself have just referred to as the remains of your family, are still at your guardian's funeral, as a

more or less curious and yet remarkably revolutionary circumstance . . . but let us get down to business: nature is infamous.
And the fact that you imagined that I myself was *probably* at your
guardian's funeral and thus in Aurach and not here . . . no matter
what, no matter where, no matter how, the human individual is
a spectre, more and more of a spectre, and human beings are
nothing but spectres . . . and the spectral life is, to quote your
guardian, a delight as a form of de-delighting . . .

If you do wish, as you say, to disperse, to give away, everything having to do with Ungenach, this will be an unprecedented
event. The legal situation is as simple as it is bewildering. The
law in question is a confused one. The facts of the matter are
unprecedented . . . I cannot call to mind a dispersal on such a
colossal scale . . .

. . . and if, as you say, you actually intend to leave today, to
leave for Chur in Switzerland,' said Moro, 'then of course the
entire matter, meaning the matter in its entirety, will also have
to be certified today . . . you are basically acting as your father
would have acted in this situation and under these circumstances . . . ' and then: 'such an untimely death as that of your
guardian is of course in reality never an untimely death . . . a person dies and thereby turns over a new leaf . . . and as everything
has of course been expressed beforehand, everything continues . . . you see . . . and as I know, there exists not the faintest
trace of sentimentality between you and your guardian . . . but I
would not go so far as to say that your relationship was exhausted
by an attitude of especially discreet mutual respect . . .

... and now that your brother Karl, that is to say, your half-brother Karl, has been eliminated'—he did not say 'murdered'—'everything is much easier . . . '

Miss Zelter, Moro's secretary, had brought in a new bundle of Ungenach-related documents, together with my lists, itemizations, preliminary estimates, etc., which I had compiled at Stanford and mailed to Moro even before my departure, and gone back out, and Moro was beginning to compare the deeds, land-register excerpts, etc., with my lists, itemizations and calculations.

'Regarding the settlement,' said Moro, 'regarding the settlement in a manner of speaking . . . basically everything, even on such a colossal scale, is quite simple . . . but justice reposes atop its own obstructions, it has been wholly built up atop absurd complications . . . and been entirely reliant on perplexities . . .

a gigantic dispersal,' mused Moro, 'one that is unprecedented, thoroughly uniquely unprecedented . . . yet when everything is aiming at annihilation, at the annihilation of the old living conditions, the exploration of new ones . . . you know that the news is already a couple of thousand years old for us . . . history-makers, history-fakers, *historical-change-fakers*, as your guardian always used to put it; we believe, we say from time to time invariably in a righteous tone, in a human-righteous tone, my dear Robert, that everything ought to be annihilated . . .

I was often at Ungenach even as a child,' said Moro, 'and when your father was governor of our state, I was still constantly coming and going to and from Ungenach. With my mother. With my sister. On hot summer evenings . . . At one point your father retained twelve hundred employees in the forest, you know . . . that was really not that long ago, now that I think back on it, eight hundred farmhands . . . stable hands, maidservants,' he mused. What Ungenach was back then, *before* the First World War, is unimaginable today. As is even what it was *after* the First World War, *before* the Second World War . . . and what, as you yourself will see, if you can take the time to read through these documents, it all amounted to . . . even your father didn't know exactly what it amounted to . . . solely and uniquely *my* father knew the particulars of everything pertaining to Ungenach . . . and then after him *I* did, but when I took over this office, Ungenach was no longer Ungenach . . .

. . . but even when one deducts everything that nature, society, etc., whatever we care to call it, has deducted from Ungenach in a relatively short time span, a full quarter of it over the course of three decades,' said Moro, 'something that no longer exists here in this state always remains . . .

this will be a gigantic dispersal,' said Moro, 'naturally there have always been changes where Ungenach is concerned, auspicious ones up until the turn of the century, after the turn of the century inauspicious ones, catastrophic ones for Ungenach naturally . . . some of them subtending, others supervening . . . basically Ungenach has always been in motion . . . your father, later too your guardian, kept the estate in motion . . . and there was no speculative element in any of this . . . to take in at a glance a thing of such bulk,' said Moro, 'is not easy for a notary, not to mention for its owner . . . in point of fact, these bundles of papers' (all of which are labelled UNGENACH) 'are the most interesting ones I have in the house,' said Moro, 'without a doubt . . . Ungenach meant everything to my father; I myself often devote my nights exclusively to studying these papers, if I am unable to sleep or purely out of interest in the business of the estate . . . these nights have made clear to me many things, all these connections . . . and the decoding of all these connections pertaining to your family, for one can infer therefrom the diversity and multiplicity of directions from which your family has arrived as well as the multiplicity of directions in which it has departed . . . these often remarkable representatives of this family, all these life-craving Zoisses,' said Moro, 'whence they have arrived and whither they have departed . . . over the course of centuries . . . for in point of fact the Zoisses have made history, made *this* history, the Zoisses have single-handedly made this history . . . and to be sure you as a Zoiss are also making history and making *this* history . . . even when you are in America you are making the history of the Zoisses and the history of our state . . . these bundles are to be sure only a fraction of those that pertain to Ungenach or to the Zoisses . . . to your family, as I said, to this name Zoiss, as I said, but also to mine, Moro, which names have always been tightly bound up with these papers . . . many things pertaining to my father, pertaining to my mother, to your father and your mother, to your half-brother Karl, are becoming clear to me thanks to these papers . . . and above and beyond that the history of the entire state, this fundamentally completely unintelligible landscape, population, etc., . . . of the Salzkammergut, of the Innviertel, of the Traunviertel, of the Hausruckviertel . . . this entire population structure, this Upper-Austrian existence . . . why, just consider in isolation the part pertaining to the timber industry, or even, say, the salt

industry . . . the cement works, the foundries . . . the salt and timber industries used to make full-fledged history, and the Zoisses
of course, as you know, have almost single-handedly made the
history of this town . . . this history is based on the Zoisses . . . it
is all here, to be read through in and from these papers, all several
thousand of them, this history,' said Moro, 'that basically no
longer interests you in the slightest, can no longer interest you
in the slightest . . . besides, given that you are on the verge of
making your temporary residence in America into a permanent
one . . . this history no longer interests you, that is the truth, and
of course we also hear,' he said, while leafing through the papers,
'when we prick up our ears, we also hear subversive voices,
whenever we open the newspapers, etc., voices of subver-
sion . . . the words use of force permeate the columns of the
front-page articles . . . in a righteous tone, a human-righteous
tone . . . filling out hollow spaces,' said Moro, 'with revolutionary
cement, as your guardian put it, you know, cementing them
through and through with revolutionary cement, as your guardian put it . . . hollow spaces are supposedly everywhere nowadays
. . . you see, in all honesty, a person like me does not grow weary
of a job like mine; on the contrary, he devotes himself to it
day in and day out with an ever-increasing inquisitiveness and
capacity for effort like a legal dispensation regulating his understanding; on the one hand he must set off, secure, segregate
himself from other people; on the other hand, to a super-
constructive extent, my dear Robert, he must intensify,
strengthen, his contact with other people with an ever-increasing
pertinacity . . . that such a constant alternation between one hand
and the other is taxing, that it indeed often stretches a person's

capacity for endurance to its utmost limits, is easy to con-
ceive . . . existence is always extreme and the effort to exist is
intrinsically quite megalomaniacal . . . but it is a genuine art,' said
Moro, 'to segregate yourself a hundred per cent from other
people and at the same time to merge with them a hundred per
cent . . . but indeed the whole of humankind has been living,' he
said, 'in complete exile for the longest time; it has bowed and
scraped itself away from nature, shooed itself away from her in
a manner that is extremely ingenious precisely because it is
extremely ruthless towards humankind itself; you see how it is,
my dear Robert . . . and the concept of nature, you see—the concept of nature as we still understand it and as the people to whom
we listen, as the newspapers that we open, the books, philosophies, etc., understand it and fashion it and employ it and
practice it and invariably still do so in the most absurd manner—
pretty much no longer exists at all, my dear Master
Robert . . . nature no longer exists at all . . . and who would know
this better than a Zoiss,' said Moro, and: 'these new tendencies
on the other hand, *trans*tendencies, all of them still versions of
this old concept of nature,' he said, 'anarchisms of the old concept
of nature, revolutions of the old concept of nature . . . absurd,'
said Moro, 'all of them still versions of this old concept of nature;
well, then: for the sake of revolution, till there is nothing left
but revolution, nothing left of the old concept of nature . . . and
for the sake of inventing a new natural-cum-spiritual constitution,' he said, 'naturally . . . youth paralysed in its opposition to
old age . . . annihilation,' he said, 'such that in every idiotic governmental institution hundreds, thousands, hundreds of
thousands of innovators are soliciting for custom . . . this new

natural-cum-spiritual constitution of which one hears so much
talk these days, but there's still this old concept of nature, you
see . . . products of the imagination that our oafish eggheads are
force-feeding themselves day in and day out and that naturally
must pass undigested from these heads into the populace . . . if
we look at history, we see that we are only ever dealing with a
colossal swindling of the people . . . with an obscene shambles
of huge proportions . . . naturally,' said Moro, 'we are not existing
in any sort of dormancy period and it is a good thing that we are
not mingling with our head during any sort of dormancy
period . . . indeed, we exist in an age of such elevated, nay, per-
fervid insanity, in a disordered natural nerve centre, as your
guardian put it, and to be sure, Zoiss'—he suddenly addressed
me as 'Zoiss' and not as 'Robert'—'you see that Europe has once
again donned the fool's cap and bells, the filth must pass over us
all yet again . . . every twenty or twenty-five years, you see, but
from now on in unimaginable proportions . . . in the country and
in the cities with which we have dealings, in writings, everywhere
we get to, everywhere we come to, pseudo-political infectious
diseases are rampant . . . the houses, the books, that one enters
are treasure troves for the collectors of political perversity . . . the
nation-states, Europe as well as America, are masturbating, and
once again we are seeing throughout the world an infamous
ineligibility for marriage making history out of their
excreta . . . governments are depleting themselves in vulgar oral
propaganda . . . Communism, Socialism, Democracy are risible
manifestations of a global masochism . . . soon on earth, or let
us rather say in nature, which we do not understand, on this
sadomasochistic spherical substance, I suppose, we will have no

more than two or three hermetically sealed iceboxes, so-called continental refrigerators, into which the past as well as the future will have been placed for long-term preservation.

to disperse this estate,' said Moro, 'completely disperse it, because to you—as you say, precisely because you have gone to America, in the midst of this anachronistic ethnic ordure,' said Moro, 'as we now see—because to you Ungenach no longer means anything, Ungenach for you is a prepotent burden, as you put it in your letter . . . and because you are unfortunately teaching chemistry there, at Stanford, because they did not let you teach chemistry in Austria, because they expelled you with your brain from your fatherland, because they expel all people of genius, whose heads are too big, by which they mean that the contents of their heads are too big for this tiny, absurd country . . . this colossal legacy is of no use to you . . .

to disperse this monstrosity,' said Moro, 'for in point of fact in dispersing Ungenach, which means nothing but annihilating Ungenach forever, you will be annihilating not only Ungenach . . . if as I believe—as indeed I can plainly see now that you are sitting across from me here—you are going to go ahead with this plan, you will also be annihilating everything associated with Ungenach, annihilating this entire history, as I have already said, actually annihilating this entire history, annihilating everything, I repeat, everything . . .

but let us get down to business,' said Moro, 'if we carry out this dispersal, it will easily take up the rest of the present year, partly because I of course have to obtain an acknowledgement of receipt of a bequest, etc., from all these people to whom you are giving away parts of the estate, from all of these remarkable, and for the most part absurd, beneficiaries of dispersal, but of course I do not doubt that all of these people will acknowledge your bequest to them . . . it will easily take up the rest of the present year, for the wheels of justice turn with punishing sluggishness . . . we shall thoroughly discuss all of this today, and then you will sign a form granting me power of attorney,' said Moro.

'The unfortunate thing is that you have gone to America and that is why this unfortunate event has now taken place . . . '

Moro said: 'And as I know, it was by no means by chance that you went to America, just as it was not by chance either that your half-brother Karl, that thoroughly unfortunate individual, went to Africa . . . that you both left Ungenach, left Ungenach, basically, in order to destroy Ungenach . . .

but precisely such unfortunate circumstances as your undoubtedly admirable appointment to this position at Stanford are annihilating everything . . . naturally the whole business still requires a detailed correspondence between you and me; we shall have to correspond a few more times regarding this business, for the simplicity that we now perceive is a thoroughly erroneous one, my dear Robert, you must yet brace yourself for a succession of vexations, for a dispersal, or more precisely a dispersal of such unimaginable proportions, entails the greatest vexations, as you must readily imagine, because you are after all as well acquainted as I am with all these people who must receive something . . .

. . . and so ultimately those who have fashioned revolution and those who have not fashioned revolution, who have fashioned what they believe is a new natural-cum-spiritual constitution, one that they believe is diametrically opposed to the old one, a constitution completely opposed to the old society, who have made what they believe to be the science, the work-force, etc., best suited to them . . .

. . . as we go through life laden with the whole perverse history . . .

. . . these heterogeneous people, on whom you are bestowing these bequests,' said Moro, 'this concept astonishes me,' he said.

'Actualization, my dear Robert, is of course the destruction of actualization, but we are now fashioning this revolution, they say, because it is our revolution, they say, at certain times they call it this fantastical revolution, at others this actual one and vice-versa,' Moro said, 'and we have to pay heed to revolution, not on account of what naturally follows in the wake of revol-ution, they say, what revolution ought to have as its object, naturally must have as its object . . . actually has as its object . . . and whither it has led and naturally leads . . . we are fashioning this revolution, they say, because we must fashion it, because there is always a good reason for fashioning a revol-ution . . . because we are living in a period in which once again today revolution *must* be fashioned, they say, what has been thought is being fashioned out of thoughts, they say; we are fashioning a reality that is the actual reality . . . and because we must all dwell together in a period in which *we* do not think, in which nature thinks and in which we do not rule but, rather, in which nature rules with absolute authority . . .

this pre-summer,' said Moro, and looked down at the street, 'these ever-unchanging goals in nature . . . this annually recurring worldwide rash, this natural arrogance, a theory of colour as a form of natural arrogance . . . this is all once again at its acme . . . as you can see, this is all for the benefit of the pure dermatologists of creation,' and then: 'for the benefit of your philosophical masochism, Zoiss,' and I thought, at certain times Moro says 'my dear Robert,' and at others 'Zoiss' and that this always has a completely determinate meaning; he said, 'this masochistic philosophism, which you have become habituated to in America, which you have cultivated very successfully there . . . Of course nature,' he said, 'is as you know a natural phenomenon itself, etc. . . . and yet,' he said, 'it is absolutely devoid of anarchy, which is quintessentially human, absolutely human . . . anarchy/politics/man/nature, etc.,' he pondered.

'If I were younger,' said Moro, 'and if my name were not Moro, if you were older and your name were not Zoiss . . . for over time,' he said, 'you see, the forces that one must bring to bear and rally, simply in order to bring oneself, to rally oneself, through the next day, will come, my dear Robert, in connection with which it must be remembered that the idealistic is nonsense; such colossal forces, forces which your late guardian always used to talk about, forces which those people who do not think about them—those people in opposition to whom one must constantly develop, constantly renew and intensify these colossal forces, etc.—are incapable of forming any idea whatsoever; this colossal energy must be pitted against the vulgar, the unconditional, the abject, against human nonsense and against human brutality, do you understand, my dear Zoiss, quite apart from the exertion, the mania for struggle against collegial vulgarity, wretchedness, etc., all of it lethal . . .

today everything suffers from intelligence, not from poverty, and age is antithetical to youth, which I am inclined to describe as a thoroughly natural megalomania, age being by contrast a repulsive megalomania . . . Whither is one to look to avoid succumbing to despair? What you are doing, my dear Zoiss is to be sure also an act of resignation and probably a much more shameful one at that . . . for this dispersal, this, as I see it, colossal dispersal . . . because this developmentalization, socialization, national, and therefore global, senilization is so absurd . . . for in the wake of Socialism and Communism we are in a precise sense perishing together, as we perished in the wake of the Imperial and Royal dispensation, *because we must perish*, for ultimately everything is oriented towards going under . . . as Communism and Socialism are of course solely and merely global depressions, global perversions . . . but the waves of global depression and the waves of global perversion must pass over us . . . over everything . . . this has basically been the preoccupying fact of my entire life, under the auspices of which fact I have carried on my entire existence, more or less intently . . . and thus also to see this dispersal, which you are planning to carry out like a criminal carrying out his crime, like the condemned criminal carrying out the lifelong prison sentence that has been imposed on him, and to carry it out, I am inclined to say, with the greatest possible degree of emotional poverty, for as I see it, you evince not the faintest stirrings of emotional activity . . . So you are liquidating

Ungenach, fine . . . but the fact that you are dispersing Ungenach and thereby annihilating it . . .

The walkers,' said Moro, looking down at the Kirchengasse, 'are the most sensitive anachronisms while they are taking their walks; they are the most rational of the most irrational people, as well as the happiest of the unhappiest people; possibly they are, my dear Robert, but one mustn't tell them that they are the most rational among of the most irrational people, the happiest of the unhappiest people . . . one mustn't accost walkers . . . who roam about with some or with no piece of business in their heads . . . first and foremost,' said Moro, 'human beings make an enormous production out of staving off boredom . . . one form of pointlessness pitted against another form of pointlessness . . . they roam about the forests, they roam along the lakeside, into the gorges, out of the valleys, and as you know, as many as two billion human beings roam about day in and day out and unrelentingly . . . such that they can basically exhaust themselves completely in eating and sleeping . . . very often, precisely because I was preoccupied with the Hisamgut here, my father would first and foremost go with your father for a walk in the Hisamgut . . . through the Kammerhofgärten . . . Laudach, Langbath, Grünau, Lindach, Rutzenmoos, Aurach . . . in point of fact these walks would lead to conversations pertaining to Ungenach . . . and it also often seemed that these conversations were completely unfathomable . . . your father,' said Moro, 'and also my father, were walkers, walkers to their very cores, and yet for all that they were not anachronisms; nor for that matter was your guardian an anachronism either . . .

walking and thinking, this simultaneity,' said Moro: 'I observed it in your father as well as in your guardian, as well as in my father throughout their lives. I myself do not take walks. On account of this more than of anything else I aroused the distrust of your father, as well as the distrust of your guardian, incidentally . . . walkers distrust people who do not walk, who are non-walkers; the anachronisms, etc. . . . and so this lovely landscape, this landscape of ours, is permeated in the most remarkable fashion by an unrelenting distrust, in truth an omni-obfuscating distrust; a delicate tissue of distrust of non-walkers by walkers permeates this landscape.'

'Thus friendships between walkers and non-walkers are unthinkable . . . as is friendship in general,' said Moro. 'When I take a look here at your itemization pertaining to Lindach, or pertaining to the Hisamgut, I really do think that friendship is impossible, for these two estates have been proving for centuries that friendship is nonsense . . . in point of fact nonsense, my dear Robert . . . by which I mean that when one begins to scrutinize a friendship, searches for its causes, its effects, its goals, and ultimately searches *through* it, it comes little by little to explain itself away, it evaporates into a nightmare, Zoiss, and one sees that it no longer exists at all, that it never existed, and if one is intelligent one is cheered by this realization . . . the realization that it like everything else was a gruesome and at the same time immoral means to an end . . . your guardian often used to put it that way: we are persistently, and every now and then *in*sistently, pursuing the means to an end . . . everywhere nowadays one sees routes,' said Moro, 'routings, as your guardian always used to call them,

but reality bypasses, the future bypasses these routes, these routings, these often far-too-philosophical routings, street networks;
reality and the future quite simply *give them the cold shoulder*, as
people very scrupulously say . . .

In the majority of faces there is nothing but stupidity, and it
is stupidity to surmise that there is anything other than stupidity
in all these faces or to look for anything other than stupidity in
them or to wish to fathom anything other than stupidity in
them . . .

on account of which the masses have an absolutely stupid
face,' said Moro, 'for stupidity running into the billions is naturally unbearable . . . but as we are seeing once again right now
stupidity also has the means, and hence the strength, the power,
my dear Robert, to extinguish, extinguish and annihilate, everything that is not every bit as stupid as itself . . . even though,' he
mused, 'stupidity and poverty are two completely distinct concepts, they nevertheless both lead to the same goal . . . if we were
to give our decided opinion about all the ruling phenomena of
the present, we would be obliged to say that never before
has everything been so grotesque, although of course all
the ages one right after the other have always been grotesque . . . undoubtedly,' said Moro, 'that is also relevant to the
discussion; as your guardian put it, it is much more lamentable,
more abominable, which is to say, more unprofitable, to annihilate the inherently detested human beings of a higher order, who
are on the point of dying out and who have already been virtually
annihilated, than to avail oneself of the common and base ones,
in other words to guide them, to introduce them to the higher

things, possibly to their own higher essence, which is to say to prime them in such a fashion that the common and base beings are transformed into beings of a higher order, the higher beings into higher ones still, etc. . . . but human beings are besotted with the road to ruin,' said Moro, 'and democracy, in which the biggest blockhead has the same right to vote and the same weight in voting as the genius, is a form of lunacy . . . to this extent the world,' said Moro, '(if this term is still even remotely tenable), a world that was always on the verge of ending, has by now already outlasted its end, for the end of the world is piece of adolescent nonsense . . .

The distances between human beings are increasing as the isolation of the individual is increasing . . . human beings,' said Moro, 'aim at entertainment and are consequently ancient history, in the baser strata of life as well as in the higher strata thereof; anyone who comprehends this is quite simply nauseated by it, and there is nothing truer than when somebody says that he is feeling nauseated.'

The Austrian, Moro reckoned, was constituted in such a fashion that, because one still feels sorry for this beaten-up nation, there was no use in constantly referring him to Mozart and Stifter, to the insane Raimund and the maddish Wittgenstein, in referring him to nature, which undoubtedly could not but be an Austrian nature . . . 'Nowadays nobody credits us with either the power (and the culture!) that we do not have, or the power (and the culture!) that we once had, or for the most part never had at all, because nobody credits us with anything at all any more.'

The causes of anxiety, Moro said, if we research them, are perfectly clear, but that still always leaves the question of what anxiety is.

Seen in this light, concepts are the things that stand at the farthest remove from us. In this respect, concepts are no concepts.

'Every life is a logical conclusion in itself,' said Moro, 'as your guardian quite often said, in every individual there is synthesis . . . and the philosophies—not the philosophers, mind you—philosophize, in other words, abadumbrate, abacinate, abominate, annihilate . . . '

Generations of ashamedness are followed by those of shamelessness.

'Your guardian put it this way: everything goes to show that *we* are shameless.'

'Spirit, the perversion of spirit, a mirror image of all brains,' said Moro.

'As your guardian very often used to put it: to enter large areas of space, to enter ever-increasingly large areas of space, to enter space itself ultimately . . . but to whom are you saying this in such a way that everything is as incomprehensible as possible . . . for we incessantly talk like this, like impoverished people talking about their property, which they no longer have (or ever had!), the elderly about their youth, philosophers about their philosophies, statesmen about their states, etc. . . . .

and the greatest misfortune,' said Moro, 'has been brought into the world over the course of centuries by the Church, the Church, in which time and again, throughout these centuries, the same spiritually deleterious drama has been staged, this congenial drama of profitableness, which in all these centuries has never been withdrawn from the stage even once, has kept having its run extended ad infinitum,' said Moro, 'and ever since the world began, so to speak, the Church has been in the repertoire, in the playhouse's repertoire, my dear Zoiss, and every couple of hundred years something is crossed out of the play, and something is added, but it is always something insignificant that is crossed out, always something insignificant that is added, always something that the church cashes in on at the box office . . . these worldly wise stage-directors of the faith,' said Moro, 'stage-directors of our religion . . . and this is all done with the tacit approval of the general manager, of the general manager of the theatre of the faith . . . and year in, year out, this entire circus has never wanted for spectators or popular acclaim . . . even or precisely in hard times the Church has played to a sold-out house . . . wherever we look . . . there are myriads of analogies,' said Moro, 'pathological neurological processes . . . an arrogant global confusion in the form of a century.'

'Let us get down to business,' said Moro, 'so then your cousin Linus is to inherit the Peiskam Forest in its entirety . . . '

This morning the Simplon Express, according to Mrs Morath, has in conformity with tradition collided with a freight train; moreover, two of the eighteen fatalities so far reported were residents of Chur.

The really exciting thing, Moro reckoned, would be to plunge one's head—he said one's own unique head—first into physics, and then into metaphysics and thereby to grow old and waste away first in a physical fashion and then in a metaphysical fashion.

Mrs. Morath asks whether I have any desire to go into the 'courtyard', but I have no such desire.

'... one must bear in mind that the Kammerhofgärten alone are easily worth two million,' said Moro, 'if your cousin Franz Schabinger inherits the Kammerhofgärten, I shall no longer be permitted to go shooting within their limits . . . together with them your cousin Schabinger will acquire the properties on the Hongar . . . I have written all this down in draft; Miss Zelter will draw up the final copy later . . . this is of course an unprecedented dispersal,' he said, 'as far as real estate is concerned, woodlands, agricultural lands, etc., quarries, cement-works, town houses, pieces of furniture, etc. . . . I suppose I shall catalogue the furniture and other movables separately . . . just as I shall of course also catalogue the parcels of woodland separately from the agricultural properties . . . speaking, as we just were, of the Kammerhofgärten, do you know that according to the district agricultural office's latest survey they amount to eight hundred and twenty and ahalf hectares . . . I quite often went to the Hongar with your father; we would head up there first thing in the morning and often not head back down till late at night . . . basically the whole business is superlatively simple, because I have prepared it all with superlative exactitude and organized it all quite thoroughly; all along Miss Zelter has been doing an enormous amount of work for me, and outstanding work at that, I must say . . . do you know that including

Ungenach there are only eighteen estates containing large forests left in the whole of Austria?' said Moro, 'and after this dispersal is carried out, we shall be down to seventeen . . . the domain of the law quite often embitters and cripples those people who come into contact with the domain of the law, cripples and embitters them from the outset, and for their entire lives . . . then we have,' he said, 'the Hisamgut and the Wöllergärten, Rutzenmoos and the woodlands on the Grasberg . . . I must say, your cousin Süssner, who of course is now incommunicado,' Moro did not say: 'is now in the Stein Penitentiary,' 'struck me throughout my life as an exceedingly suspicious individual, and my suspicions were eventually borne out . . . basically all these people study medicine only in order to extract money out of those of us whose carcasses have suddenly started causing trouble . . . don't let me get started on the subject of medicine! . . . you are giving Süssner the most beautiful of all your manors, I must say, and also, mark my words, one of the most productive ones, as I am now seeing here . . . Süssner's father was the worst doctor imaginable . . . these people were always suspicious in the highest degree . . . and Süssner's mother was what your father would have termed a tarted-up, bigoted country whore . . .

In point of fact once many years ago now, rumours were circulating that my father had had an affair with Süssner and that under the pretext of having to visit the district agricultural office he had used to go into town once a week to meet Süssner, and that Süssner in turn had used to come from town once a week to Ungenach, specifically to the hut on the Gmös Moor . . . Moro spoke not a word about the rumour, although I had been waiting for him to start speaking about it, because he knows all about the rumour.

'So Süssner is inheriting the Hisamgut,' said Moro; 'this lamentable fact gives me reason to doubt the seriousness of your dispersal . . . fine,' said Moro, 'the whole business will naturally gobble up an enormous sum in governmental fees, an enormous sum,' he said several times, 'not to mention the incredible amounts of tax that all these people will have to pay, these people whom you, as I am just now realizing, are about to be so incredibly absurd as to . . . fine' said Moro, 'you yourself will not lose a penny through this dispersal thanks to the sale of the property called Unterach . . . by the way, I have already got this sale underway . . . the whole Unterach business will possibly be settled as soon as next week . . . once I have sold Unterach, I shall be able to finance this dispersal without a hitch . . . but naturally this dispersal will entail on your American-residing end a legal form-induced nausea that will overwhelm you without warning, a legal form-induced nausea of unimaginable proportions . . . by a rough estimate, the part of the Hisamgut to the north of the Ager alone is worth a million two hundred thousand, by a rough estimate, but its actual value is probably a great deal higher . . . but as for Süssner,' said Moro, 'Süssner of all people . . . but of course you are not listening; we have now already been talking to each other for nearly three hours, and more than anything else we have been talking about Süssner and other people like him, these people who live in conflict with the law and to whom you are granting bequests . . . but you are not listening.'

Life was direct, death indirect, 'as your late guardian put it,' said Moro.

As far back as anybody can remember, the Moros have always been notaries, lawyers, all of them residents of Gmunden.

The Moros' house in the Kirchengasse is one of the oldest in town, older than the five-hundred-year-old pharmacy next door, and certified to have been for more than two hundred years in the possession of the Moros, who came from Tuscany. One of my ancestors hired a Moro from Florence as a stable hand. Like everybody else in Gmunden, the Moros have tended to be sickly but to survive into old age. 'Your guardian once opined that a person left his house,' said Moro, 'as if for the purpose of being put on trial, of *submitting* to a trial, to a trial by jury, and that it was only after having been condemned, in every case condemned,' he said, 'often to many years of arduous imprisonment, of endarkenment in solitary confinement, naturally, that he returned home.'

Beneficiaries of my dispersal:

I.

Schabinger (Kammerhofgärten, Property on the Hongar)

Gruber (Rutzenmoos)

Goi (Wöllergärten)

Söllner (Langbath)

Lent (Vöcklaberg)

II.

Schrögendorfer (Wankham/Peiskam Forest)

Stadlmayer (Brauching)

Plöchl (Houses in Matrei)

Süssner (Hisamgut)

Hippel (Neukirchen)

Anschütz (Loifarn)

III.

Hennetmayer (Hildprechting)

IV.

Ehrlich (Town houses in Vienna)

Sinzheimer (Parz)

Palant (Gmös)

Zumbusch (Murschalln)

V.

Turegg (Lagross)

Dapprich (Holzkrumm)

Köchert (Altmünster)

Rosenstingl (Traich)

Schickinger (Föding)

Spalt (Kirchham)

VI.

Hufnagl (St Konrad)

VII.

Pauser (Weiermayer grist mill/sawmill)

Tenants to receive compensation as a result of the sale of the Unterach Estate:

Asamer

Radner

Reisenberger

Kothmeier

Maxwald

The following are notes regarding the beneficiaries of my dispersal that I have jotted down for my own use: Schabinger says in English *old growth, broken forest, low bush,* talks only, if ever, about woodlands and forests, about wood, types of wood, the export of wood, about the kapok tree, the librodendrus, second growth, scorched areas and clearings, etc. . . . during the summer, racks his brains about the winter accident victims in his woodlands, whom he then describes with his great aptitude for description . . . in calmly composed sentences developed out of his own outlook, and in his listener's presence, he fashions the daily routines of his workers, co-workers on his estate, into a plotline that is faithful to the facts (Father). Strives, in accordance with his upbringing, his origins, for ever-greater sagacity, classification of reality. An autodidact in geometry, higher mathematics.

Gruber, a chess player, has 'discovered one of the best possibilities for living' (Father). An admirer, a collector, of chests of drawers from the Josephinian period. 'Ever-deeper strata of worlds.' 'Infinitude as a concept of old age.' A clear form of consciousness. 'Death as natural science juxtaposed with life, life.'

Goi, calm and composed, sequestered from all of us during a christening reception at the Fersenagut just above Brixen, in his father's library with the philosophical fragments of Kierkegaard, while we in our exuberance were making a great illumination in the vineyards . . . an antipathy to all forms of sudden accostation, accostedness. His sisters objected to his Styrian-tailored loden apparel. At my father's funeral, probably also at my guardian's funeral, he wore over these self-same loden clothes a black cape, a garment originally worn by south-Tyrolean shepherds. On that occasion, at the cemetery in Aurach, he invited me to the grape harvest at the Fersenagut in late autumn, an invitation that I declined, because I was preparing to leave for Stanford. I perceive that he observes a dangerous inner restlessness in me.

Söllner, aged twenty-eight, four sisters, all unmarried, older than him, completely isolated from the outside world; his life on the shore of the Langbathsee. (Echolalia, catalepsy, stupor, echopraxia.)

Lent, born in 1931, working as a foreman at a quarry after his abortive studies in the natural sciences. Two children. Exceptional musical ability. (Autism.)

Schrögendorfer, Linus, completely isolated due to carelessness, living in the Peiskam Forest. ('I understand nothing.') Autism.

Stadlmayer, born in 1917, enjoyed my father's confidence, as well as my guardian's; superintendent of the Brauching cement-works. Perceives his own children as strangers, his wife as a source of nausea. 'Because I am naturally wrapped up in my job.'

Plöchl, Konrad, trauma. The cause of the unfortunate incident on the Brenner Pass in which his parents were killed was a torrential downpour.

Süssner, Stein Penitentiary

Hippel, Georg, who lost his wife and children while exiting Gemona del Friuli. A monument has been raised at the site. They had been on their way, in a new car, to Padua by way of Venice. Works as a warehouseman in Neukirchen.

Anschütz, Josef, born in 1941, who was obliged to pursue a legal career after his father, who was a lawyer in Loifarn, shot himself. Married a timber-merchant's daughter from Feistritz who died last year. Lost everything in speculative investments.

Hennetmayer, Karl, 'natural theologian' (Father).

Ehrlich, Franz, philosopher, Vienna.

Sinzheimer, Ludwig, forester's helper whose mother has retired to Tarvis (now located in Italy). From there, in weekly letters (printed family coat of arms: two crossed swords above a trout), his mother tells him, her Reschen-resident son, about long walks through the Val Canale, about her memories of her first and third husband. She lives with the second one. She often writes about gorges, weird animals, buried treasures, about adulteries, disasters, earthquakes, imbeciles. Her hatred of all things Carinthian, Italian. 'Ultimately a victim of her own solitude immured between lofty rock faces.' (Father)

Palant, Franz, a day labourer at Kircham with whom I went to elementary school.

Zumbusch, Churean uncle, philosopher, mill-owner, toll-collector on the Splügen Pass.

Turegg, born in 1938, scholar of the theatre, proprietor of a bank. His studies were not pursued to their conclusion.

Dappich, Ferdinand, restlessly shuttling between Graz and Rome. Has never had a trade or profession. Is in possession of an already virtually exhausted fortune. His mother is an epileptic.

Köchert, Robert, son of a brewer. Author of an 'ichthyology'.

Rosenstingl, born in 1926 in Krakow, surveyor.

Schickinger, construction worker. Conversation in the Kammerhofgärten.

Spalt, urban garden-labourer, lives at 23A Am Hochkogl, Gmunden.

Hufnagl, geneticist. An article on 'Induced Mutation Events', another on 'Methods for Detecting Mutations in Chromosomes and Gene-Types'.

Pauser, Sergius, philosopher, man of the world, mystic.

The following persons will receive sums of money from the sale of Unterach:
Kulterer, Very Reverend pastor, Vöcklabruck;
Hofrad, August, woodworker in Reindlmühle;
Pius, Ferdinand, journeyman miller in Aschbach.

Additionally:
Fabian, Titus, day labourer, currently in Garsten Penitentiary;
Absam, Nikolaus, foreman, currently in Suben Penitentiary;
Ritzinger, Viktor, currently in Göllersdorf Penitentiary;
Kobernausser, Justin, currently in the Steinhof mental hospital.

'When we,' your guardian said, when we were in Hongar on Corpus Christi that one time,' said Moro, 'are standing on this undoubtedly loveliest of all rising grounds in the Alpine foothills and looking down into such a landscape from such a height, you see, we instantaneously think about everything that is happening in this landscape, that ever happened and that ever will happen there, everything, do you understand, my dear Robert, the entire past and present and future that pertains to this landscape . . . it is not possible to look down into this landscape in any other way.

. . . in history we never see anything but particulars, possibly only the most ancillary particulars, as your guardian put it. We recapitulate, reconstruct the nondescript as history . . . in the midst of human beings we know well enough how to observe human beings, but we are not as good at studying them and are downright bad at judging them . . . one must emerge from the position of observation into the position of judgement . . . To be sure, approaching the object, thus said your guardian, draws us away from the object . . . as we desire rest at certain times,' said Moro, 'and restlessness at others . . .

so I quite often spent time in the company of your guardian, when the opportunity to do so was auspicious, for the sake of hearing such maxims . . . admittedly,' said Moro, 'in his last days, in the progressive course of his illness, which, as we now know, he subsequently, and not without putting everything pertaining to Ungenach in order beforehand, evaded more or less without any fuss . . . of course I was the one who wired you the news,' said Moro, 'as your notary,' he said, 'I was obliged to send that telegram, a fact that gave me much food for thought, my dear

Zoiss . . . in point of fact a colossal confusion began to reign at Ungenach as soon as the death of your guardian was discovered . . . but as you know, your guardian had no influence whatsoever on your father's will, in which everything was awarded to you and of course to your half-brother Karl . . . and after the death of your half-brother Karl, etc. . . . '

'Your guardian was extraordinarily well informed and precise in the matter of Ungenach . . . and of course since the death of your half-brother Karl you have functioned as sole heir . . . Your father, just like your guardian, hardly ever, as I know, talked about the condition of the estate . . . and you yourself have taken no interest in Ungenach either . . . which of course also accounts for your intention to liquidate Ungenach . . . for the fact that such a liquidation is even possible . . . just now you were surprised at how big it all is, and Ungenach today is not more than half of what it once was . . . and the fact that you refuse to allow yourself to be overwhelmed by such an enormous vastness . . . and that you are retaining for yourself only thirty thousand dollars with which you plan to support yourself. . . because you believe that thirty thousand dollars will suffice you for the future . . . of course I do not know what America means to you; I myself have never been to America . . . and I am also very much the sort of person who could never live in America . . . who could not even live just anywhere in Europe, do you understand, who can exist only here in this landscape, which is his own . . . and how remarkable it is that both of you, your half-brother Karl and you, have forsaken this country and gone away, your half-brother Karl to Africa, and you to America . . . because here you were not afforded any possibility of developing yourselves,' said Moro. 'I do not understand,' said Moro, 'why this country lets all the people who amount to something run away, expels them, brazenly propels them to other continents . . . I do not understand this . . . but naturally this country is dominated by the most appalling conditions, conditions that one cannot imagine, an unimaginable feeblemindedness is winding the key of the machinery of our government . . . granted, much and indeed everything in this country is laughable . . . pathetic of course, theatre . . . such that one is quite conscious here that one is dying, withering away, that one has decayed and must wither away . . . and such that it chills me to the bone whenever I think about it, my dear Zoiss . . . but everything is helpless and powerless . . . when one cannot sleep under the terms of such appalling arrangements, one cannot fall asleep and says to oneself that our fatherland is no longer anything but a base, brutal idiom of idiocy . . . of shamelessness . . . the children,' he said and looked down at the street, 'play and live completely beside events, while the adults are brutalizing, withering away, are actually no longer present at all . . . whoever succeeds in writing a comedy or a full-fledged farce on his deathbed has achieved the full measure of success. The insane asylums, your guardian said, confine themselves to confining insanity that is universally tolerated; criminal insanity is found only outside their confines . . . but everything is nothing but insanity.'

KARL'S PAPERS

. . . I shall never again—this is my definitive decision—go back to Accra and thus I shall never again go back to Africa; the circumstances do not permit a return of my person . . .

as recently as yesterday, as I was already busy packing up my things, and even as recently as during my conversation with Robert, I believed I would still be capable of departing tomorrow; all signs pointed towards my departure then; I also wrote to McDonald in Dakar, and to Stirner and Reitmayer the engineer, that I would be arriving on the 24th, and so yesterday I thought that I would be departing tomorrow, that I would be returning to where I have been working for the past three years . . .

. . . without achieving any results; the mere fact of having to recognize the futility of such work in Africa . . . and via McDonald in Atakpame (Ghana), that I would then be resuming my work next week, when I had left off doing it on the day of Father's death . . .

that it is obvious to leave Ungenach, certainly in consideration of my brother Robert, who is teaching in America, who is also leaving Ungenach once again tomorrow, going back to Stanford . . . but whereas I am constantly working for a worthy purpose, Robert is oblivious of any sort of worthy purpose . . . it is precisely this worthy purpose, along with worthy purposes in general, along with the whole concept of purposiveness in general, that I have been unrelentingly pondering in recent weeks, months, probably even years . . . because I am imprisoned in the notion of being able to continue to exist only in Africa, just as Robert believes that he can continue to live only in America . . . for I have always believed that Africa is my only possibility of existence . . . that in Africa alone is possible what has become impossible for me in Europe . . . it was this notion that allowed me—given that I was completely unprejudiced, because for so many years I had been totally alone, alone beside my parents, as I am now alone beside my guardian, and beside Robert—to enter into a partnership with McDonald and to accept the position proffered to me by McDonald . . . because I am suddenly no longer able to bear the thought that Robert is in America and is making the greatest headway there . . . headway of a most personal nature . . . and with what intense enthusiasm did I accept the position offered to me by McDonald . . . right up until the last instant, from the instant at which I arrived in Dakar, then in Accra, onwards . . . but today I see that I can never again go back to Africa, just because my brother is at Stanford and is going to stay at Stanford, or at any rate in America . . .

and now McDonald is rightly demanding an explanation; I must deliver up a description of the circumstances that have arisen here and that are suddenly prevailing here with colossal violence, deliver up such an impossible justification . . . but I cannot explain Ungenach to McDonald, explain anything connected with Ungenach, explain where I would have to begin and how . . . when I simply cannot begin to devote myself to all our connections, which are all lethal connections . . . but in a telegram I can at least formulate my awareness that I shall never return; I can at least send off an illuminating communication . . . and I see that nothing whatsoever can be made comprehensible, that the method by which we proceed from Ungenach, by which we approach Ungenach, is lethal . . . and that what I am saying must remain impervious to understanding.

Frankly speaking, in the basely carping tone of a political stump speech on my own behalf . . . everything is a lack of understanding, because nothing can be made understandable any more, when naturally everything is in the process of being liquidated, on account of which I can no longer sleep.

Ungenach
17 March '65

That everything was merely an attempt to make themselves understood, while I was wasting away at Ungenach alongside my parents and alongside my brother and alongside my guardian and alongside everybody else. Or they suddenly do away with themselves, because they can no longer tolerate the rhythm that prevails here, or they become absorbed in a frenzy of reading. In an insane vehemence.

Because I must always infer everything from particulars and conversely infer particulars from everything. Human existence consists in consciousness of the fact that nothing comprehensible can be made material, in ignoring this fact, in therefore vegetating in consciousness, not in a relatively simple life as a minimal existence.

In point of fact I cannot even explain to myself why I am suddenly never going to go back to Africa again. And why I am remaining in Ungenach, which I know spells insanity (fluctuating insanity).

Never again going where my only possibility of existence is to be found, or remaining here, where there is no longer anything for me, because I believe I must remain at Ungenach . . . for in truth it was only my realization, never mind where or when, that I would suddenly have to be at Ungenach again someday that impelled me to go to Atakpame.

As far as I know, I have never managed to make myself understood to McDonald. The nature of the matter is as follows: if I were to say that there might very well come a moment when I would have to return to Ungenach . . . if it were possible at some point to make everything clear to myself, even everything pertaining to me along with everything pertaining to everybody else, at some point, in a single thought, this clarification would naturally signify an understanding.

But for this a third person would be indispensable, indispensable as a neutral brain, which person or thing naturally does not exist.

I keep telling myself that I ought to go back to Africa, but I am not going back.

Everything here and in general suggests that I ought to return to Africa immediately, just as my brother is returning to America immediately.

Everything is a motivation.

I myself have had my nose put out of joint, have been taken aback in an instant. By myself.

Therefore I am sending McDonald a telegram notifying him of my resolution without further comment. For that my conduct will entail a breach of contract—that this conduct of mine *is* a breach of contract!—is clear to all parties concerned. As I knew nothing and at the same time everything, I committed myself for a period of eight years.

And I have served for three of those years.

And I have always believed I would be able to attain an always-increasing intensity, and not only in my thoughts. Able to be responsible. And to be responsible specifically in the manner McDonald expects of his colleagues.

And we have always attained the utmost, and at the same time, nothing.

It is we who are the failures.

Given that I must utterly and completely abandon my work and the work of my colleagues to the judgement of McDonald, of McDonald who possesses superlative powers of judgement, in retrospect . . . such that all our exertions have ended in a catastrophic depression (Reitmayer). We have consistently and repeatedly been working our way ever further away from this depression. As we have indeed consistently and repeatedly got out of the bed that is this self-same depression and washed ourselves and dressed ourselves, partaken of food, consorted with women . . . in the conviction, the actuality—not the feeling—of futility.

But the fascination with futility (Reitmayer) has not allowed us to arrive at a full-fledged state of despair.

The entire time I have been preparing an attempt at an explanation, although I know that an explanation is impossible. But since we immediately become incapable of explaining anything when we think we ought to explain something, to vindicate ourselves, etc. . . . because wherever we look, the neutral brain fails to appear, everything is so much stage-scenery in the absence of the neutral brain, even though this neutral brain is the central point of reference of everything, as I have no choice but to conclude . . . philosophical irreparabilities, inversions as a condition.

To McDonald

. . . I got out of bed tonight and have been intending to write this letter, but the tranquillity that prevails here and that has always prevailed here at Ungenach has made it impossible for me to write to you . . . lying in bed, I made a rough draft of the letter, but then, when I got up, I was unable to write . . . and I have since been repeatedly unable to write; in the light of this you will see that my situation is an aggravated, if not a hopeless one, and rest assured a desperate one . . . I intend merely to say that I shall never again go back to Africa, *I am not permitted* to go back there again, I am no longer at liberty to do so . . .

You will be unable to picture Ungenach to yourself, to picture the buildings and this colossal despotism of real estate that grinds down human beings . . . the fact that our father no longer exists means that Ungenach no longer exists . . . my brother is going back to America tomorrow, as you will have learnt from my reports; for years now he has been teaching chemistry at Stanford in the USA . . .

This letter would not have presented such difficulties to me if I had sat down immediately after supper still carrying in my head the sentences that had occurred to me during my father's funeral at the cemetery in Aurach, where it was so hot that it reminded me of Atakpame . . . right there and then my brother consented to my not going back to Africa; he recommended my going to America . . . but doubtless it would be impossible for a person like me who, in contrast to my brother Robert, has learnt absolutely nothing, to get a firm footing in America . . . for my brother Robert's actual imminent return to America is a different matter from my counterfactual imminent return to Africa . . . we are very much of two quite mutually distinct natures . . . Atakpame means something different from Stanford.

But you cannot demand any explanation from me if you also feel it desirable for me to explain things to myself now . . . the tranquillity that prevails here has always killed everyone and everything . . . but I am also not permitted to go back to Africa on account of the poor state of my guardian's health.

During the night I enjoyed clearer versions of these very thoughts.

Such that, before I began this letter to you, I began one to Dr Stirner (who hails from this area, as you know), in which I am requesting the few personal belongings that I have left behind in Atakpame, books, photographs, letters, etc., down to which my emotional and intellectual environment has dwindled in recent months . . . in point of fact, in Africa I have discovered—thanks to you alone of course, albeit also thanks to the mediation of Dr Stirner—what I sought in vain for so long in Europe. I have discovered the possibility of elbow room, elbow room that I have allowed to expand without interruption in Africa, for in Europe I no longer enjoyed any elbow room until the moment when I met you in Brussels and signed your contract.

A contract whose terms committed me to eight years, whereas I have served only three years. From my non-fulfilment of the terms of this contract spring two difficulties, the greatest of which are in my own head . . . I am scheduled to arrive at Dakar on Tuesday, at Accra on Wednesday, but I shall not budge the slightest distance from here. It is as if I could never again budge the slightest distance from Ungenach, as if it had instantly become impossible for me to remove myself from the buildings in which I have taken shelter . . . and I shall in all probability remain at Ungenach for all time to come . . . in matters pertaining to Ungenach, even the lies are true.

As is the completely imaginary aspect of things, in point of fact . . . you will rightly have come to think that I have gone mad in the interval since my departure, for nothing is easier than to go mad.

All of a sudden, thanks to these sentences, everything seems erroneous, the errors themselves seem erroneous.

But I myself am thoroughly familiar with this manner of speaking of mine, as you must know; I am therefore capable of speaking in my manner of speaking . . . if only an explanation were possible, but an explanation is impossible . . .

To Dr Stirner

. . . this familiar atmosphere, Stirner, these horrible people, these old walls, lifelong habits . . . this silence and this megalomania . . .

I am staying in my old room, in which everything is as it always has been . . . How, I think, I would often sit in this room for hours on end, motionless, incapacitated . . . would sit for literally hours on end at my desk, which is in reality my grandfather's (my maternal grandfather's) desk, and would therefore sit at it for hours on end . . . and would lack the strength to get up, I think, to leave . . . just as I cannot leave Ungenach now . . .

without reading anything, without being able to write anything at my desk, my grandfather called it a *thinking desk*, in catastrophic motionlessness, powerlessness . . . being crushed to death by the complete works of Kant . . .

How often I have sat down at this desk with the intention of developing engrossing thoughts, in other words, embarrassing thoughts, incapable of even the most trifling amount of movement in my thoughts . . .

thoughts developed during walks, thoughts that would be gone when I sat down at the desk . . . when I would approach Ungenach in the midst of a thought after a rather long walk often extending as far as the Hausruckviertel, and then as I passed through the courtyard, as I shut the gates behind me, as I opened the shutters in my room, this thought would suddenly absent itself . . . on many days I would make great leaps forward, on others I would ascertain nothing. To live for the purpose of washing oneself, of paying visits, of eating, of receiving visits, of talking, and talking about grievances or about indications of grievances over and over again . . . to talk about the causes at one point and about the effects at another and against the grain of one's own brain at each and every point . . . my dear Stirner, as you know, each and every day we have the milk that we drink at Ungenach brought up from the town, even though we have a huge dairy, because my stepmother wants this, because she wants all the meat that we eat to come from the town . . .

When I have been shut in for several hours for the purpose of studying, I dare no longer venture out of my room, because my sojourn in my room has been fruitless . . . one can spend days, weeks, on end in the company of books, atlases, precision maps, crouching down on the floor to philosophize about oceans and never-seen cities, be alone in one's room with hated writers, but one must then all of a sudden go out again and thereupon take heed not to go mad.

Upon entering my room I immediately thought that everything that I am is closely connected to this room, that I am what I am thanks to this room, and so on . . . and that it is so tranquil above the granary . . . just as it is now, after the funeral, to which a crowd of people whom I do not know at all came from every point of the compass, from every country in the world . . . I have been obliged to think about those hundreds and thousands of sleepless nights, nights into which I have crammed far too many senseless thoughts, nights in which I have read into myself that entire heap of novelistic nonsense written in the nineteenth and in the first half of the twentieth century, those unimaginably meaningless and featureless productions . . . imprisoned within my four walls, whose smallest and tiniest particulars I have been acquainted with since earliest childhood . . . reminiscence amid all these roomy irregularities . . . under the window-seats, over the chest of drawers, over and under the door, lines for my trained eye . . . lines that cross each other, that intersect, that permeate my entire memory, where I also like to stay in order to think.

At the mercy of this contemplativeness I have found my way to my very own mathematics. Unbearable midsummer nights. These fissures and incisions, from the time *before* the turn of the century, from the time *after* the turn of the century, because we are all whitewashing our living spaces . . . where the lines stopped short, went under, began again, etc., lines as elements, interconnections, suppositions . . . and I would hear everything, and I believe—because nobody had the strength for it—that I always heard everything alone. Since the stable hand was so far away that he was unable to hear the sound of the walls, to hear the decay that one incessantly hears at Ungenach . . .

Today in a corner of the forecourt I discovered the saddlery that my father bought from a farmer in Linz on New Year's Day

1934 . . . my father said some things, but *what* he said I no longer hear; now I only ever hear *how* he said things, and never *what* he said . . . how he would speak like various other people from Tyrol, as if he were speaking about our relatives in Passau . . . about their nonsensical preoccupations, and all of a sudden I saw Ungenach itself as a perfect piece of nonsense.

The mendacity, Stirner, when I suddenly saw that because my father had died all the shutters were shut and so forth . . . and when I found that the shutters in my room were shut, I got the impression that the shutters had never been opened the entire time that I had been in Africa . . . and I thought: everything really is completely unchanged: the park, the trees, the branches of the trees . . . I instantly went to the park, so deeply into it that I managed to fill it up with living beings, with actual human beings, as I ascertained, with relatives, just as one fills up a side-stage with human beings (with relatives) . . . full-fledged well-dressed human beings who, in compliance with a mise en scène no more determinate than this, were incessantly walking out of the park and walking back into the park and again walking out of the park and so on . . . I could quite distinctly perceive their clothes, their diction, their accent, Stirner. I know what they are thinking. But all these people, I thought, no longer exist. This mechanism exists, to be sure; these people do not. Laughter in the park. Depending on their frame of mind, they allowed themselves to be ordered around well or less well there in the park. Four in front of the fountain, eight behind the fountain, six in front of the tree, eight behind the tree and so on . . . I arranged it all, and it was an utter delight for me. As I step up to the window and actually look out, I ask: what has become of all these people? The unanswerability of this question terrifies me . . . suddenly my attention was exhausted, and the people had vanished from the park.

And so the park is empty; I see nothing, hear nothing.

My room is lethally unchanged.

My guardian's wife was not once in my room during my absence, I think. Paintings, miniatures, engravings, incunabula, unchanged; Venice, Padua, Mantua, Bergamot from the Nuremberg Chronicle. The laundry cabinet, the book cabinet.

The many artists that would often paint one of us here at Ungenach in exchange for a warm meal. An uncle, children. Fluvial landscapes, snippets of landscapes like a piece of the Höllengebirge, of the Totes Gebirge . . . two grandchildren sitting on the laps of their grandparents, dressed for their first communion . . . *dab-brats*, said my father disparagingly. How very little meaning have the higher or highest arts, painting and so forth, had for me; I have found even less meaning in masterworks than in dilettantish productions, for example, the painting of my Great Uncle Rainhard, a grist mill-owner and sawmill-worker, as compared with a famous portrait by Cézanne . . . our hallways are lined with abbots, bishops, a cardinal, military officers, scenes of revolution, Indians held captive at cannon-point by the English and so on . . . the ever-popular tumult of battle, the ever-popular encirclement by the army, demolition of entire nations . . . all these people, families, this whole reign of terror, out of which and into which I have been begotten as a product of contingency . . . even as a child I often pondered this terrible word *reign* as a reign of terror, and I thought that the word *reign* along with reigning itself, along with the concept of a reign, in every case signified the reign of terror.

'As we moved from German to Spanish books and authors, to French books and authors, and from French books and authors back to Spanish, Italian, and German books and authors.' Robert.

'It vexed me to be losing my way in the vitiated modes of intellection that are ubiquitously observable nowadays; I found it repulsive.' Robert.

'Circumstances are such that in their wake I shall soon cease to be able to read anything, take note of anything, regard anything as true.' Robert.

'Sometimes I leave home and wish never to come home again; sometimes I go home and wish I never had to leave again.' Robert.

'The cause of death is in myself.' Robert.

'While I was mowing at Ungenach at four o'clock in the morning I mowed the forelegs of the roe deer invisibly standing in the grass and the deer fled into the forest and bled to death there . . . ' Robert.

'If I lend an ear to their tactlessness . . . ' Robert.

. . . I was quite good at Latin, while my brother is the better mathematician.

. . . when I was bedridden for two years, Robert instructed me in the natural sciences and in English.

... his attempts at steadfast self-sufficiency, in which he succeeded and I did not.

... his eloquence in writing letters, which I do not write; the art that he was born to master and that I have not mastered.

... the fact that we both don't know what to do with our money.

To return to Stanford has not been his only way out, but my only way out has been to return to Accra.

When our father completely lost his eyesight, he believed he could see better and systematically, because all of a sudden he was beginning to hear. By switching off all the doctors he succeeded in seeing everything more intensively, albeit nothing whatsoever any more in actuality, *through his ears.*

The mention of Stirner arouses Robert's mistrust.

We talk about something or drink something or talk and drink: depression as a habit.

Misfortune as a habit.

The belief that we had a *right* to our life, *because* we knew nothing about it (Father).

To Robert

... as you are waking up you are assigned a role that you will then play for the entire day without being allowed to tire out a merry or a comic or a depressive role in real life.

you judge people in accordance with your own will, and every thought you think is a thought from which I must be excluded . . .

Incessantly and gradually using my eyes to reconstruct upon the forest floor an Ungenach that no longer exists, that in reality never existed, hundreds upon hundreds of meanings as your future life: a natural relationship.

With the untimely death of Father, to whom I was bound by a tranquil relationship of mutual trust that fortified my entire life, by a natural spiritual kinship.

Walking for two hundred, three hundred metres completely soundlessly, then while speaking into the landscape ahead of me and answering questions that one is not permitted to answer.

'When we have not spoken at all for some time, we must speak; when we have spoken, we must be silent.' Robert.

All these tens of thousands of human beings whom you perceive and who will ultimately prove to be your relatives.

Time and again the unfortunate accident in the Totes Gebirge, which, because I have read about it in the newspaper, is preoccupying me more than the other accident in the Katschberg, which I lived through.

The fascination with empty spaces, completely vacant rooms, in which a dead person is always laid out.

With Robert in the Mountains

A Fragment

When, in awareness of the fact that at the end of autumn the days are already much too short, we go quite early in the day into the forest, and thus into the gorge, for a walk; in the light of the fact that it will soon no longer be possible to take walks, we set out on walks that are doubtless much too long, walks that we only very rarely manage to complete as we have planned to do; we often no longer manage to cover even half the distance and are already tired before then and are obliged—not only owing to our fatigue but also because of the weather—to go all of a sudden into an inn or even a house that is not an inn, because we cannot make it to an inn . . . we are incapable of looking for an inn, of asking for directions to an inn, hence of reaching an inn, even though there are such a remarkable number of inns in the gorge, that one would easily estimate that every second or third house is an inn. I am familiar with many of these inns, but there are still a number of them that I am unfamiliar with, that I have as of now only heard about and not seen, let alone sought out. When I am on my own, for familiar reasons, I do not seek out an inn, but when I am with another person the search for an inn is still a delight for me in certain circumstances, and this search for an inn is often my sole salvation from a total breakdown. There are so many inns here, I say, because it is so dark. Great darkness, I say, equals a great number of inns. Doubtless we are exhausted; once again we have undertaken much too much today; our hasty, reckless, and above all self-thwarting walking is to blame for our exhaustion. We have devoted too little attention to the economy of our walking. We walk and think, but as we are walking we do not think, above all else, that we are walking too quickly as we are thinking; we think and do not observe our walking. We walk, but do not think, as if an ever-greater state of exhaustion. We believe that we are capable of walking faster and ever faster and capable of thinking and imagining ever-more intensively, capable of philosophizing ever-more intensively; without thinking that we should have walked not quickly but slowly, we walk much too quickly and thereby soon become the victims of our now-catastrophic exhaustion. Our exhaustion, I said, is very much the catastrophe that we fear it to be. We have overestimated our corporeal powers. Having drawn to a halt, I said to Robert: although there are a great many inns in the gorge, at the moment we are nowhere near the nearest inn; I don't believe we have the strength to make it to the nearest inn. The nature around us irritated us. We had been happy in its midst for two hours; now it was depressing us. It's as if all of a sudden the roaring of the water has become unendurable, the air, the rocks, have become unendurable, I said. One supposes that one can hear the birds falling to the ground like rocks. No matter what kind of house it is, we're going into the next house, I said. All houses are empty. Not all of them, said Robert. The extinct inns are falling into ruin; nobody in the gorge takes any interest in them. Once upon a time, decades ago, all these houses were inns, were alive; a remarkable, boisterous, impulsive hustle and bustle—one admittedly muted by the river water—ran the entire length of the river, of the gorge. Need I say, I said, that all these inn-frequenting people, whether they have gone extinct along with the inns or not, are related to one another? There are no longer any raftsmen on the river. Rotting millwheels, I said. Holdovers amid the entire madness. Sunlight falls on the bottom of the gorge only twice a year. Here it is as dark as can be. But not because the gorge is actually as dark as can be, but because the gorge is as cold as can be. By the time I had finished making these remarks, we had reached the mill built half across the river and half into the rocks, which is to say we had been standing directly in front of this building for some time without having noticed it until that moment. In we go, I said. The building was reminiscent of a prison. The windows had bars on them, whereupon I pointedly drew Robert's attention to them by saying: drawn curtains behind the barred windows. Initially the massive edifice seemed to be uninhabited, but a piece of laundry hanging from a broken shutter on the second floor indicated with absolute certainty that this was a building in which human beings were living. We can't go any farther, I said; we're too exhausted. Come on, Robert, I said. Let's go inside, I said. In the darkness we had not noticed that if we wanted to get to the building we had to go over the river. A wooden bridge. Let's go, I said. The bridge was only a footbridge. I led the way. What if he falls, if he falls now, I thought. Robert! I cried. I have often felt, when walking with my brother on a dangerous pathway, across a bridge, a foot-bridge, like this one leading across to this building, that he could fall headlong. I have feared this all my life, feared that he could fall headlong, fall to his death. We shall ask, I said, if we can have something to eat and something to drink. I knocked. A short time after I had finished knocking, the door was opened. We were immediately allowed to enter the house. To think that for the longest time only this single human being (the fifty-year-old woman) has lived here, I thought, as we entered the hall. On both the left and the right side of the hall there were doors leading to rooms of great and indeed incredible spaciousness. On the floor lay heaps of garments, garments reduced to rags. Actual rags, said Robert. We were supposed to follow her into the kitchen. Sides of bacon hung on a row of rusty iron hooks. We could have bread—bacon and bread. Spirits. But since we gave her the impression that we were completely exhausted, she offered us only water to drink. She gave me a knife. Robert had to catch in mid-air a loaf of bread that she had flung at his chest. The kitchen was not a place in which to spend a moment longer than necessary, she opined, and then she went out into the hall; we followed her, Robert after me. I couldn't see anything whatsoever; I was guided by the sounds I heard. We suddenly found ourselves in the room opposite the kitchen, which gave me the impression of being completely dark in contrast to the others. On the table there was a bottle of spirits . . .

(1941)

In the Human World

Actualizing propensities, desires, plans, the quest to make resting places possible without losing the distance . . . with the capacity to form sentences as they believe sentences ought to be formed, as Robert forms sentences, while he is uttering them nonchalantly . . .

Then again unusually short sentences, which re-establish the equipoise of thought . . . to speak with reference to the centre in unrelenting command of one's intellectual and corporeal powers, to silence appearances, to clarify causes and so forth . . . to deliver oneself up to childhood as a cause of death . . . to make oneself into a reality while remaining fully conscious.

Whereas in point of fact and in and of themselves, things are without cause and effect.

'My unconscious youth.' Robert.

All of a sudden, after weeks of seclusion, landscapes, cities, people, indomitability and madness surface in the brain.

The notion that I am little by little working towards an achievement into which, as Robert has put it, I shall crawl for refuge when I am older.

And studying the constituent pieces of this achievement as one would study the furniture in a building that one had purchased but not yet thoroughly inspected.

The inventory of his brain.

My memory fails whenever my train of thought suddenly preoccupies itself with me.

'The quest to locate people whom I have not seen in a long time and whose terminal illnesses are gradually thrusting themselves into the foreground.' Robert.

The older we get, the further our mental hygiene deteriorates.

A perennial course of study: my own head, my own body.

The sudden idea of fashioning my own thoughts out of my antipathy to principled madness.

Against opinions.

'On the whole, nature is a form of journalism and on many days the brain is an article deleted from the arts-and-culture section of the newspaper of nature.' Robert.

'Because I exhibit too much of myself (in myself), which everybody subsequently knows.' Robert.

One day before I am to board the tanker Cambon

Hotel Impero, Trieste

. . . I see on the floor of the lobby downstairs a heap of luggage belonging to some arriving or departing guests. I want to know what is in the luggage, even though I know what is in the luggage, that nothing else is in the luggage and so forth . . . I go into the lobby downstairs a couple of times solely in order to look at the pile of luggage, and pace up and down and await the arrival of the people who belong to these individual pieces of luggage, who are doubtless the owners of this luggage; I look on as they carry their luggage into or out of the hotel or have their luggage carried into or out of the hotel. My manner of contemplation is such a conspicuous one that it is already preoccupying the concierge . . . and I ask myself how I should respond if the concierge, who is probably younger than me, asks me why all of a sudden my person has pitched up just when a pile of luggage happens to be accumulating in the lobby . . .

I take immense enjoyment in picturing to myself the people who belong to these individual pieces of luggage one by one, in subsequently seeing these people in the flesh, the lady with the black suitcase, the gentleman with the black suitcase, and so forth . . . the cripple with the collapsible folding chair . . . I watch as all these people take up their luggage, carry it out, carry it in, as they order their luggage to be carried out or carried in; I watch the way they walk and what they are wearing, what they have on their heads, watch to see whether they use walking sticks or don't use walking sticks . . . but I have no desire to accost any of these people; I worry that somebody will accost me and so forth . . . most of the people who alight here are completely ordinary, speak only one language, evince a vulgar, primitive outlook on life . . . and it astonishes me that such a large number of primitive, vulgar people are roaming the earth, that this new community of the vulgar and the primitive is roaming the earth in such great numbers . . . in the Hotel Impero everybody who comes here, for whatever reason he comes here, alights here, instantaneously becomes as hideous as the hotel itself, everybody who comes into the Impero instantaneously takes on the hideousness of the hotel, for in the street none of these people is as hideous as he is after he has alighted at the hotel, and the longer one stays here, the more hideous one becomes . . .

(To Robert, unsent)

To Renner the physicist in Vaduz

... whether you remember my father, and if so, whether you would mind giving me a description of the march you went on with my father in '37 in Switzerland, specifically from Sitten (Sion) to Leukerbad ... my father was always talking about this march, which the two of you took through Raron, about a certain Alpine railway line that the two of you could have used but did not use ... my father often spoke of a certain mathematical problem that the two of you posed to yourselves during this march and that neither of you was able to solve ... and what did the mathematical problem centre on? And in what did the difficulty of solving it consist? Can you recall anything whatsoever about this mathematical problem? I believe it must have centred on something significant, because my late father spoke about it quite often indeed, because he was always bringing up the subject of it ... I would also like to know if on that occasion you used the famous ladders on the far side of Leukerbad, on the day of the thunderstorm ... my father often talked about these ladders, he would link them up with the mathematical problem. Please allow me, esteemed sir, to call upon you to think back on that march ... for it was as a march that my father described the excursion that the two of you undertook back then ... I would be grateful to you for each and every piece of information ... for the biography of my father, who has now been dead for fully three years, has been enveloped in great obscurity, such that, now that I finally have time to do so, having just returned from Africa, I wish to do everything in my power to impart light to this obscurity, with which I have been preoccupied for years ... and if you believe that in the present circumstances many or even most of the things you recall in connection with the trip to Leukerbad are of no significance, please bear in mind that for me everything is significant and that for me everything, and not only what pertains to this march, is of the utmost significance.

Please understand that I must initially investigate everything connected to my father, only after that can I investigate myself. Everything will indispensably contribute to the formation of my final opinion, just as everything would indispensably contribute to everything . . . but it seems to me that the experience you shared with my father during this excursion, during this march through the most beautiful stretch of land in Switzerland, and probably in all of central Europe, is of the utmost importance.

The fact that until now I have been unable to track down your address from Accra, where I am presently employed, that indeed I have been unable to track it down from here for two or three years, for I really have been wishing to get in touch with you for that long, accounts for the fact that you are only now receiving this letter.

Our name should be familiar to you; indeed, before the last war you were once our guest at Ungenach for several days . . . and my Uncle Zumbusch in Chur is no stranger to you either . . . in the meantime much has changed . . . my father is dead; my mother, as you know, died immediately after the end of the war. My brother is in America. As for me, I originally intended to study natural science, but I ended up not studying anything whatsoever, not pursuing any further education; instead I kept house at Ungenach, which housekeeping was of no redeeming value for me or for Ungenach . . . admittedly in Africa I have time to devote myself to my natural-scientific avocation, to genetic mutations . . .

Throughout his life my father perceived Ungenach as a dungeon. Everything here is being changed. My guardian, but in particular my stepmother, is changing everything . . . and Ungenach is being transformed into an unparalleled travesty of nature that I am incapable of describing. But I shall not allow myself to indulge in any unseemly digressions.

Please do not discard these lines as so much tedious verbiage; please, rather, consider that the man who has addressed them to you has read all your publications with great interest and admired them and is now awaiting a reply that is of greater importance to him than any other reply ever could be.

What happened that night you spent with my father in a village above the ladders of Leukerbad? Why had you arranged to meet my father in Sitten of all places? My father had then stopped at Brieg on his way to Gorzia and Cormons. And what, above all, did it have to do with the mathematical puzzle with which, as I know, my father was preoccupied until the end of his life? There are many things pertaining to my father that I know nothing whatsoever about and that likewise pertain to this march . . .

(Unsent)

... had written today to Widmer the actress that her presence at
Ungench was always welcome, that we were setting aside a room
for her and looking forward to the pleasure of her company
... that whenever people gather here at this thoroughly wintry
place called Ungenach, they crave a beautiful, varied summer,
in other words, the most relaxing distraction, in other words, the
merriest of moods ... I would have liked to call on her at the
Josefstadt, but the play in which she was supposed to star tonight
has been cancelled and no other has been scheduled in its
place ... and so, I had written, out of my disappointment at not
having seen her I was going to take a walk through those parts
of Vienna with which I was still unacquainted, from Josefstadt
to Leopoldstadt and from Leopoldstadt to Brigittenau and over
to Döbling ... where, I wrote, I was going to call on a friend, a
certain Hager, a conductor.

To Köchert, a jeweller in Altmünster

Why did you talk, as we walked through the woods, about
politics, when you know full well that when I am walking
through the woods, especially when I am walking through the
woods with you, I take no interest in politics, that the woods are
no place for political conversation, not even for political conversations with oneself, as instanced by the one you carried on with
yourself yet again the day before yesterday ... but also the ones
you have carried on with me ... have you not been carrying on
your political conversation for the longest time, for the past two

decades? . . . Just as my guardian has been carrying on his philosophical one? Just as my father has his been carrying on his
philosophical-cum-mathematical one?

As you know, I have been ill for several days and have, while
bedridden, taken an interest in prehistoric man of the tertiary
period, and also in Peking Man, in the entire fossil record; this illness has been immensely beneficial to me . . . especially in relation
to the visual perception of objects, the art of visually perceiving
objects. Everything within me is oriented towards this art . . .

Unease

I put on my jacket, I take off my jacket, I put on my trousers, I
put on my jacket, I take off my trousers, I put on my trousers, I
put on my overcoat, I put on my shoes, I take off my overcoat, I
take off my shoes, I take off my jacket, I take off my trousers,
and so forth.

Childhood

Robert and I could be distinguished from the other children by
the ordinariness of our apparel, not by our abilities, disabilities,
or by the attributes of our upbringing.

. . . even though in point of fact Ungenach is situated in the
very depths of the lowlands, we had always lived under the
impression that its buildings had been erected on a hill, even
though in point of fact Ungenach is situated at a lower altitude
than all the buildings that do not form part of Ungenach.

Subterranean corridors run beneath Ungenach.

It is remarkable, said my father, at certain times in the autumn—when one is beginning to open and to peer into old trunks, chests of drawers, etc., because one is starting to feel chilly and one is starting to think of winter clothing—to happen upon the wedding dresses of long-dead spinsters every so often.

'The winters were long and cold, the summers hot and short.' (Father.)

As I read these notes, I am getting the impression that everything was very much as I described it, and thus that it still is as I am describing it, as the others have described everything, and as I myself shall someday describe everything on the basis of all these notes, and yet not one word of it is true.

We wait in the waiting room and when our name is called, called by a doctor, we no longer remember what we have been waiting for.

Parallels.

Death makes a dead person into a dead house in which one searches for him, an empty world in which one searches for him . . .

. . . I believed that my unease would cease, that at last I would be at ease; now my unease is greater, my solitude definitive.

I listen to Handel's *Suites for Harpsichord* played by Christopher Wood, and I am happy.

My thinking leads to causes; one ought not to bring a philosophical-cum-medical captiousness to bear on Father's death as Robert repeatedly insists on doing, one ought not to make his death into a pretext for speculation along lines that are alternately philosophical, medical, and medical-cum-philosophical, when we are after all quite simply dealing here with persons as culprits . . .

To my stepmother

. . . this house, all these houses were in the course of your marriage to my father transformed into your house, into your houses and the landscape into your landscape, into your plane of consciousness, from the moment you inspired my father to enter into this marriage and overpowered Ungenach and knocked out my father, the most magnanimous human being imaginable, and became the rigorous queen, the disastrous queen, of this Ungenach, an Ungenach which for centuries on end had embodied an entirely different concept, a concept diametrically opposed to what Ungenach has become today; no sooner had you got Ungenach in your clutches and subordinated it to your schemes and calculations than with incredible celerity you reached your goal: the destruction of our property, of our autarchy, of our existence, of everything that Ungenach had ever been until your entrance on the stage of our history. In the year in which you embarked on your trail of destruction, two, three years after the death of my mother, you succeeded in making Ungenach, that locus of liberality and humanity and culture and all the superior qualities of our manorial class—a place that I must say was very much in step with the general trend of human development—into an unprecedented wasteland of natural and intellectual desolation and devastation, an inferno of tastelessness, as Robert himself once termed it, in which people such as

Sophie, our cousin, a person who, being a finer artistic creation
than a mere wastrel, was diametrically opposed to you, was no
match for your coarseness, depravity, cunning and monumental-
ity, who before her Ungenach days was uncommonly cheerful,
and who at Ungenach was then bound to perish, gradually, pro-
gressively perish via exposure to all our neglectfulness and
intellectual frigidity and inhumanity, to our difficult essence that
is obscured and obfuscated over long stretches and eventually
obscured and obfuscated completely; who was bound initially to
be alienated, to lose her bearings, and eventually to be killed off,
lethalized. You too hated Sophie and made this hatred of Sophie
and of all of us who believed we would be at home forever at
Ungenach into a mania, eventually into an infamy, into a perverse brutality, a brutality that is convulsively disruptive and that
I have never managed to discern in any other person I have ever
known, and you have built up your entourage by persecuting
ours . . . I shall not take the liberty of enumerating here the names
of all the people who have not only Sophie but all of us on their
consciences, the people who hunted Sophie to her death. But just
like you, all these polluted individuals live very well at Ungenach
with the consent of my guardian, and they will continue to live
at Ungenach for some time to come . . . The cause of my father's
death is therefore no secret, there is nothing mysterious about
his death, nor about the death of Sophie, who was worried to the
bone by Ungenach. To be sure, I am by no means absolving
myself of responsibility here and I shall emphatically add that
she also suffered under the sway of my proscriptions and pre-
scriptions . . . the farther away I am from Ungenach, from the
theatre of all our horrors, the more terribly ashamed I am of the
fact that what has mortally wounded me is affording you a sense

of relief. Nothing would be easier than to adduce particulars
upon particulars against ourselves in this letter and subsequently
to fashion these particulars into an indictment of ourselves, but
it is ridiculous to deliver ourselves up to a court in which we ourselves are judge and jury . . . But how might such a sentence be
passed on you, in particular on you, to keep everything from
turning into a comedy? Now Ungenach is completely at your
mercy, and every single part of it already bears the features of
your person; one can look at or reach for whatever one likes at
Ungenach and one will see something repulsive, one will touch
something unnatural, your handiwork, you . . . slowly, with the
constant support of my unsuspecting father, you thrust aside
everything Ungenach once was, thrust it aside and into the background and eventually down into the abyss . . . To think that
when I told you to your face that you had lowered Ungenach,
which had once maintained the highest standards, to the basest
level, that you had first transformed it into a house and then a
home of tastelessness; from afar, long before they ever catch sight
of the place, prospective visitors to Ungenach can fairly smell
you and your tastelessness . . . no sooner has one emerged from
the thickets of the forest, than one sees and notices this tastelessness, at Ungenach everything is tasteless . . . the outer walls, on
which you have painted your tastelessness, the bay windows, the
eaves, which you have pasted over . . . when one walks into the
courtyard, throughout which you have caulked in and painted
on and nailed down and set up your tastelessness, one realizes
that today Ungenach in its entirety is an orgy of tastelessness . . . an Ungenach dumbed down to the level of the

boneheaded stylistic criteria of the present . . . one observes with increasing disgust that thanks to you, vulgarity and irreversibility has penetrated Ungenach and is penetrating ever deeper, and that thanks to you Ungenach has been transformed from a *nature unto itself* into a *grotesque artificiality*, in which the very air that one breathes is imbued with tastelessness . . . but I suppose that these accusations no longer have any meaning, that they have come too late, that they no longer have any purpose and are only ridiculously indicative of something that basically nobody sees, because those who could see it no longer exist at all . . . a new era, this era that wipes away everything that is of no use to it, an era of superlatively incredible tastelessness, has exterminated and wiped away all of them . . . and when I told you to your face everything that I am writing to you—told it to you with this calmness in my countenance that is bound to strike you as being incomparably vulgar, vile, nay, basically illegal, and that you, who fear nothing, fear—your face remained fixed in an attitude of incomprehension, of incomprehension and immutability incarnate . . . and you mindlessly said, as you always have said on every possible and impossible occasion: let us proceed to today's agenda . . .

(sent)

In '63

. . . when I come back to the house, I hear that Sophie is dead . . . a week later I leave for Paris; Robert travels to Vienna, Robert is travelling to Vienna and will spend a year in Vienna, while I am spending a year in Paris, whereas we were conversely planning for Robert to travel to Paris and for me to travel to Vienna . . . I stayed in the room belonging to Miss Gussenbauer the physics graduate, read Montaigne in the original French and began, over the course of a long winter, to take an interest in Socialism and Communism . . . incredible news of a philosophical nature, contact with those whom father termed the character assassins of history, Marx, Lenin . . .

. . . the newcomer to Ungenach notices Ungenach only once he is standing directly before it; he is suddenly standing, after walking for an hour through the woods, before the outer wall, before the locked gate, and it often happens that even when he is expected, and even if he attempts to make himself noticed, he remains unnoticed for quite a long time and so keeps standing there before the gate and is not allowed to enter . . . since the death of my father, the gate has been kept locked by order of my stepmother and will open only when the exogenous, extramural individual has proved who he is and that he is welcome . . . but the majority of people who try to get in wait in vain . . . they are either not heard, or they are heard and not allowed to enter for some other reason . . . but the arrival of an outsider who wishes to enter Ungenach is an extreme rarity, for outsiders are not invited by my stepmother to Ungenach, and thus no outsiders are ever expected at Ungenach, and anybody who is not expected is not allowed to come in here (or to come in from out there), but let us suppose that today the gate were suddenly opened to an outsider and he were then to come in here (or come in from out there), he would inevitably get the feeling that he had stumbled into some perverse scene of horror, not, as he would have done years ago, into a natural artistic event . . . one way or another, he would feel that he had stumbled into an anachronism whose intrinsic as well as extrinsic cohesion would be bound to bewilder him, would be bound to remain inaccessible to him . . .

. . . in which everything that we hear, read, write, say, is always being sealed off, brought to a close. Ungenach: the means of unobtrusiveness to the end of unobtrusiveness. Inculcated illnesses. Feebleminded nature.

. . . fearlessly seeking out out-of-the-way settings, being in cities, on ships, in the company of human beings . . . present via absence, unassailable, in my observation of all possible human beings.

A natural tribunal.

My life as a logically consistent digression from my life.

A predilection for comedy: mortal terror.

Father's funeral

To avoid despairing completely, I ran constantly to and fro between the gamekeeper's house, in which he was put to lie in state, and the hall, in which our relatives were sitting or standing around or pacing up and down, all of them together comprising a nervous funereal congregation. Once I even counted my steps

183

between the gamekeeper's house and the vestibule. Abruptly halted several times, each time occasioning a stabbing pain in the back of my head. My mental condition has deteriorated. Although the viewing of my father's corpse has become a compulsive habit for me, today I have all day long been obliged to think about his description, his opinion of the relationship between him and me, between me and him and between Robert and him and vice-versa and between all three of us . . . I have managed to bring his notebooks into my room, agitated, in constant fear of being discovered. The difficulty of conveying his notebooks into my room was so great because the house is populated with so many people and all possible people are walking up and down the corridors . . . a hundred and thirty-eight notebooks in all . . . apart from this, I was constantly worried about being discovered by Robert. The mechanism of the house has become a mechanism of exhaustion since the arrival of the mourners, of the Italians, Portuguese, Poles, Russians, Bavarians. Father: 'Thought Number One: I can cram everything into my brain. Thought Number Two: From this brain I can extract everything.' Whereas a completely empty brain does not yet signify complete painlessness. 'My brain, into which I look *straight* down.' Father.

'The discovery that my brain works soundlessly.' Father.

In my father's notes descriptions of his life incessantly alternate with descriptions of his death.

'Lethal objects.' Father.

I read: 'I find myself in the midst of committing a thought-crime . . . how many people have I spoken to merely for the sake of hearing their voices, in doing which I have rendered myself unintelligible to them. Judgements. Mass graves in my brain. My head is as light as all of humanity.'

Robert reeled off an amazing description of our family. His high intelligence came to light with especial prominence in his characterization of my father. He is absolutely uncompromising. What he sees tallies precisely with what is. A ruthless orchestration of his thoughts. Self-evidence in the confusion of interconnections, thoughts, possible ways of orientating oneself, etc. . . . his manner of speaking: clarity even when he must employ it for the sole purpose of clarifying our bitterness. He elevates everything to the level of a reliable statement. He said, 'Your cerebral sensitivity,' and so forth. He notices everything, other people notice nothing. Father's death came as no surprise to him. Let death not come as a surprise.

In connection with Father's death

Shortly before three o'clock I was rudely awoken by a noise coming from the room adjacent to mine, the room assigned to the Portuguese man.

I believed I could hear the Portuguese man pacing up and down in his room; at length I heard him opening the window, then shutting it, then opening it again, then shutting it again and so forth. These noises suggested that the Portuguese gentleman was in a nervous frame of mind. I got up and began likewise pacing up and down my room, and all of a sudden I realized that I was pacing up and down in my room in exactly the same way that the Portuguese gentleman was pacing up and down in his.

This realization caused me to stop pacing and start straining to hear the noises that the Portuguese gentleman was producing while incessantly pacing up and down. As I was listening, I suddenly noticed that my sense of hearing had attained a painful, astonishing, and yet alarming degree of precision. The natural conditions of Ungenach encounter my will and thereby enhance the precision of my instruments of thinking and feeling in the most valuable fashion. I was seeing the Portuguese man, even though I was only hearing him. Hearing how he then suddenly emerged from his room and went down to the library and paced up and down in the library . . . all this suggested that he was the only person other than me who was not sleeping . . . now he was pacing slowly, now quickly, now on the right side, now on the left side of the library . . . from time to time he would stop, and I would picture to myself *how* he was stopping. Now he is standing before *Mayers Konversations-Lexikon*, I thought . . . he must have taken a book off the shelf . . . so he's reading *while standing still and while walking*, I thought . . . I did not know that this Portuguese man, who speaks German well, could also read German . . . at length I could no longer endure being in my room and I went down to the library and asked the Portuguese man what he was looking for in the library in the middle of the night. 'I don't know,' said the Portuguese man, 'nothing.' His German was impeccable. *I saw* that the Portuguese man had been unable to endure being in his room any longer, and it occurred to me that his room was situated opposite the hunting lodge, in which my father was lying in state. And I said to myself that the door of the hunting lodge was open and that two enormous candles were burning and that the Portuguese man was probably irritated by these burning candles. 'You can hear the murmur of the people praying,' said the Portuguese man. 'First I shut my window, and that sufficed, and I fell asleep, but then I woke up again, and I drew the curtains to no avail.' He could not sleep with the curtains drawn. 'I have been lying awake in bed the whole time,' said the Portuguese man. It was 4 a.m. 'Probably it's a nervous reaction,' said the Portuguese man.

3 Jan. '66

. . . I am still reading about Father in the newspapers. I hear myself incessantly discussing the costs of the funeral with Robert . . . I hear about how the beer-haulers are changing the blocks of ice underneath the corpse, which is frozen solid, twice a day, how the house is filling with all those people with whom I have no relations, but who are nonetheless all related to me, as I now know.

4 Jan.

From Brussels

We ask, but we receive no answer. We keep asking. Life in its entirety consists of nothing but questions, because we only ever exist where we keep asking questions but keep receiving no answers. The fact is that I exist because I ask and receive no answer . . . I feel the energies that I have undoubtedly been accumulating . . . it may very well be the case that man is nothing but an observer of nature, not its judge, which he has no right to be . . .

P. S. In the morning visited the famous collection of instruments in the Sablon.

7 Jan.

In Accra

Four thousand eight hundred crates of medicine counted, lists of contents verified. Muggy. My people are restless, not working, talking about the murder in the Marketsu. Two letters. One to Dakar, where McDonald is laid up in hospital, the second to Gmunden, to the Raiffeisen bank branch. I put my head in order, I put my room in order. Vice-versa. Father's maniacal devotion to order. Aversions. Nausea. Cortisone.

17 Jan.

Atakpame. With Stirner. Conversation about Robert Walser.

21 Jan.

I hear that our people, Hiller, Reitmayer, Nikisch, have been killed . . . we drive to the site, into a forest near Manso, and we find our people. With their heads bashed in. They hacked off the engineer Reitmayer's arms and legs and his penis . . .

The police are punctilious. At the behest of the authorities in Accra the bodies are being conveyed first to Salpont, and subsequently to Winneba. Telephone conversation with McDonald. I'm afraid, I say. Nothing in reply to this from Stirner.

We children, Robert and I, had to hold our tongues when we knew more than the adults, I said; we were permitted to speak where and when the adults were unafraid of us. Nothing in reply to this from Stirner.

23 Jan.

Karl's death

Moro: 'Last night I could not stop thinking about how arduously the legal situation would have developed if your half-brother were still alive . . . what an unfortunate individual, I could not help thinking, these conditions . . . out of fear, I must say, for politics is more or less nothing but madness.'

Ungenach

Park. Avenue. Precision: manor house, farm buildings. The dank ground-floor rooms, the arid rooms upstairs. The absence of dogs and cats, although once upon a time times dogs and cats were absolute rulers of Ungenach. Monotony as a cause, as an effect, the understanding as an investigation into the aetiology of an illness. The total practicalization of all concepts. The three pools, the three fountains in the three pools. The competing, fairy tale-telling grandmothers. Mortuary studies. Religious cures. The wastage of strong affection, aversion, etc.

The sudden entrance of the huntsmen, the piles of trophies in the courtyard.

Thunderstorms, thunderstorm moods. Poaching, leukaemia among the young huntsmen. Infections caught during the hunt. How people have coped with the war at Ungenach. Time has always been reckoned in terms of All Souls' Days. A few personal belongings. Infamy. We describe ourselves completely naturally. (Father.) History. A lack of understanding. Whenever we have travelled elsewhere, it was always only in preparation for returning to Ungenach.

My Uncle Zumbusch comes back to Chur and tells me about the funeral ceremony.

Throughout the ceremony, all eyes were, naturally, according to Zumbusch, pointed at me. At the absent one.

We went to a tavern, did not discuss Ungenach.

He takes me to Zurich.

Never going back.

Collingwood's *Despatches and Correspondence*.

'The raw materials of death.' (Father.)

Moro: ' . . . this humidity, limewater. Pathogenic qualities. To be obliged to exist, even to meditate, in odious surroundings, means unease, incessant confrontation with repulsiveness, unnaturalness, with injustice, with the chaotic; vis-à-vis nature, it means confronting her pathology of death, vis-à-vis human beings it means confronting their existential dilettantism.

'One wakes up and awakens into vulgarity and into baseness and into stupidity and into weakness of character and starts thinking and thinks in the midst of nothing but vulgarity, baseness, stupidity, and weakness of character. In nothing but the pathology of death and existential dilettantism. One hears and sees and thinks and forgets what one is hearing, seeing, and thinking, and grows old—each of us in his own innate fashion—in loneliness, incapableness, shamelessness.

'The notion that life is a dialogue is a lie, as is the notion that life is reality. Although it is not chimerical, it is very much only a misfortune in the form of infamy, a period of horror that, regardless of its brevity or longevity, is composed of melancholy and the begetting of discontent . . . only causes of death, effects of death, that run into the billions . . . we are dealing here with a colossal intolerance of creation that renders us ever-more depressed and bitter and ultimately kills us. We think we have been living, and in reality we have already died. We think that the whole thing has been an apprenticeship, and yet it was never anything but nonsense. We look and we ponder and must keep looking on all the while that everything we are looking at and everything we are pondering eludes us, and the world, which we have intended to rule or at least to change, eludes us, and the past and the future elude us, and we elude ourselves, and in the end everything becomes impossible for us. We all exist in a catastrophic atmosphere. Our predisposition is a predisposition prone to anarchy. Everything within us is permanently under suspicion. Where there is feeblemindedness, where there is no feeblemindedness, there is insufferableness. The world, from out of which we also gaze at it, is basically made out of insufferableness. The world is always insufferable by us. Our endurance of what is insufferable is a lifelong talent for anguish and sorrow possessed by every single one of us, a couple of ironic elements within each of us, an irrational idiom of idiocy; all the rest is slander.'

TRANSLATOR'S NOTES

PAGE 3 | The Ortler is the principal mountain of the range known in English as the Ortler Alps. The village of Gomagoi marks the beginning of the usual ascent of the Ortler along its North Ridge, also known as the Tabaretta Ridge. As the Scheibenboden is evidently a patch of level arable land situated at some point along this ascent, in stating that the Scheibenboden lies beneath the Ortler massif [*Ortlermassiv*], the narrator seems to mean merely that it is at a substantially lower altitude than the mountain's summit, not that it is at the foot of the mountain, let alone at the foot of the entire range.

PAGE 11 | The Payerhütte is a permanent climbers' shelter on the ascent along the North Ridge.

PAGE 90 | Strux: a kind of Austrian folk costume prevailingly consisting of leather garments.